# Roots and Wings

## by Jakub Herzig and Lena Allen-Shore

**Shengold Publishers, Inc.**
New York

ISBN 0-88400-087-7 [Hardcover]

ISBN 0-88400-085-0 [Paperback]
Library of Congress Catalog Card Number: 82-60602
Copyright © 1982 by Lena Allen-Shore

Published by Shengold Publishers, Inc.
23 W. 45th St., New York, N.Y. 10036

Printed in the United States of America

# Roots and Wings

**by Jakub Herzig and Lena Allen-Shore**

BOOKS BY JAKUB HERZIG

Nous ne sommes pas des heros
With Honor
Macevot
Black Devil
Steps in the Journey of the War
Jaslo
The Wrecked Life

BOOKS BY LENA ALLEN-SHORE

L'Orage dans mon coeur
Le Pain de la Paix
Ne me demandez pas qui je suis
May the Flowers Grow
Langue Universelle (Fraternité et culture)
The Singing God—Le Dieu qui chante

To the victims:

*They touched the heavens*
*with their wings*
*while remembering*
*their roots.*

# Table of Contents

# A Reminiscence of My Father

There are millions of stars in the sky. The strength of their light reaches far into space and time even after they expire. On earth there are people who, like the stars, leave a light that survives their physical existence. This light burns with a delicate but inextinguishable flame in the memories of those who knew these truly noble individuals. This light does not disappear either in time or in space. There is a mother who will tell her child about a good man. The child will not forget and the light will remain in his mind.

Among the people who left such a light after they disappeared, was my father, Dr. Jakub Herzig.

# Author's Note

This book is an attempt to recapture the lives of a few of the millions of Jewish victims of the Holocaust, lives which otherwise might be forgotten.

The idea of such a memorial originated with my father, Dr. Jakub Herzig, soon after the end of World War II. Some of the stories which follow were written by my father between 1949 and 1951. Those by me were written in the fall of 1981.

The stories written by my father are based on true facts which were related immediately after the war by people who witnessed the lives and deaths of the victims.

The stories written by me describe the individual traits of character of people whom I knew and whom I loved. Some of the situations which I present are based on facts; for the rest I decided deliberately to use the mode of fiction because available information about these people was incomplete.

Why the title ROOTS AND WINGS?

I love the trees. The trees remind me of men. The trees have roots and want to live. All these people who perished cherished their roots and wanted to live.

I also love dreams. I am alive and sometimes I catch myself dreaming the dreams of other people who do not exist anymore. I feel as if I am wearing wings, a pair of wings created from the dreams of those who allowed me to express their longings and their visions.

I know that every man is different, but I also know that every man belongs to the family of man. I feel a sense of belonging to those who disappeared and to those who are alive today. I often think of those victims of the war who went into the gas chambers and vanished in smoke, who were shot and buried in mass graves—victims who left no trace, no name. Often I listen to their whispers in the summer breeze. The summer breeze is the only carrier of their existence.

I think not only of the lost lives but also of the lost dreams, because each dream of man is as important as his life and each man in his life tries to make his dreams come true. The wings of dreams of the others, who believed that it was worthwhile to struggle for a better tomorrow, make me strong.

The victims vanished, but the summer breeze will never vanish and will always carry whispers about the sun and happiness, whispers of lovers who kept their promises to love each other until death and beyond death. And in the summer breeze there is the laughter of children who never grew up. I think of people whose names are forgotten. Each man, each child had a name, each had a pair of eyes and a beating heart—each wondered about the world and each of them had feelings. Often when I feel the sunshine, I try to imagine that in the rays of the sun there are the warm feelings of the victims. I don't want to believe that nothing remained after them. There must be something that remains. In the air, the forgotten dreams and sunbeams vibrate with the warmth of unforgettable feelings.

The bodies were burnt and went into the air with the sun; the feelings met the sun on the horizon.

When I watch crowds, I find fascinating the different faces, different expressions, different movements. Often on a busy street I look at people and try to discover the mystery of their beings. A mother holding the hand of a child, a man touching the arm of a woman beside him, a smile, open for me the worlds of people's lives. Consciously, I feel a tremendous sense of belonging to the human family and subconsciously, after surviving the war, there is in me a certain fear for each human life—I really care.

I care for each human life and because I care for each human life I wrote twenty stories about people who loved life as I do: Roots and Wings."

Lena Allen-Shore

Philadelphia, Pa.
June 8, 1982

# STORIES BY LENA ALLEN-SHORE

*In memory of my uncle,*
*Emil Goldman*

# An Afternoon in the Pharmacy

Emil was standing near the window. He was thirty-eight years old, of middle height, and built like an athlete. His eyes were dark green, his hair brown with some grey in it. His complexion was fair. There was a little mole on his right cheek. His lips were nicely shaped, his nose was small. Emil's face was pleasant and friendly, and even when he didn't smile there was a hint of a smile in his being when he looked at people. At the moment he was preparing a cough medicine for an old man who was supposed to arrive in a few minutes. His hands, used to holding the big and little bottles, were firm and strong. Although Emil was a pharmacist, he was also a farmer—his whole family were land owners, involved with working with the soil.

Emil loved the land, the outdoors, and horseback riding but most of all he loved people. Being a pharmacist allowed him to be with people. Now as he finished typing a little label on a portable typewriter and glued it on the bottle, he was looking forward to the old man's visit. He glanced out the window and saw two German soldiers walking down the small, quiet street. They laughed loudly. They reminded Emil of the fragility of his existence.

I know that today I am here, but I don't know where I will be tomorrow or if I will be anywhere tomorrow, he thought. But immediately he scolded himself. In my family we were always optimistic, and why should I now think about the worst?

Memories of the not-too-distant past crossed Emil's mind. Before the war he had leased a big pharmacy in the market square and there were always people coming in not only for medicine but just to visit, to talk. He was then his own master with always two or three people working for him. He remembered how happy he had been when he had signed the lease, how proud he was to be independent. It had not been easy for him to finish his studies after the First World War. His sister Lusia had given him a lot of courage, insisting that he had to finish when, at one point, he wanted to quit. He was really grateful to her. Emil also had a deep affection for the city where he lived. Brzezany contained an interesting mix of Ukrainians, Poles, and Jews, and Emil had friends among all of them. How often in his former pharmacy a Ukrainian teacher would meet a Polish judge or a Jewish lawyer. And they would discuss all sorts of issues, even delicate ones with unremitting courtesy, because of the place, because of this pharmacy where Emil kept an atmosphere of understanding.

On the days when the peasants came to sell their produce in the market place, Emil had many customers. He knew them all, the Yvans and Petros, the Ians and Stefans, offering him eggs instead of money, and sometimes, nothing at all. They knew that if they needed a prescription, Emil would accommodate them. Perhaps for this reason Emil never seemed to have enough money. People used to say, he had an "open hand" and if somebody needed something, *pan aptekarz* (master pharmacist) was always prepared to take a few *zlotys* from his pocket and help.

Emil was so immersed in his thoughts that he hardly noticed the two soldiers entering the shop. One of them greeted him in German and asked for directions. Emil explained as best he could, then went out the door and pointed the way. Only after the soldiers left, did Emil permit himself to think: They were polite. They didn't shout, they didn't give orders. Now that's a surprise! He returned to the shop, looked out the window and saw the sky. He was amazed at the tranquility of the afternoon. He felt lonely. He was sorry that he could not go home. He wanted so much to talk to his wife, whom he had married only a year before the war. He had wanted to have children—he loved children, but because of the political situation, his wife had persuaded him to wait. Still, on this fall day in 1942, he regretted that he had none. But did he really regret it? "The children are in danger—in greater danger than the adults," someone had said only the day before. Emil was very fond of his nieces and nephews, especially Albin, his sister Hania's son and Rena, the daughter of his sister Lusia, who had encouraged him to have a profession. Where are they now? he wondered. He didn't know about Albin; Lusia and her family were now living as Christians. Maybe they'll survive the war, he thought.

Emil thought that he should do something, perhaps go away. But where? How could he leave Brzezany? He was attached to this place, to this soil, to his friends, to the big lake on the edge of the city where he spent many beautiful hours swimming. He had never really wanted to travel, he was content where he was. And if he fled, what would be the right direction? He thought about the two soldiers; they had just asked about a certain road and he had pointed it out. If only he could ask somebody for the right road that he should follow. But he could not. Besides, if he left the city, there would be no one to help Jews obtain medical supplies. He was the only Jewish pharmacist still working. He had considered living like Lusia as a Christian, with false Christian papers, but had quickly given up the idea. He didn't know how Lusia did it. She never knew how to lie, he thought. In his imagination he saw Lusia, her husband Kuba, her son Adam, her daughter Rena, and he wondered if he would ever see them in reality again. The sky darkened. It was five o'clock. November is dark, thought Emil.

The fall had never bothered him before. He liked all seasons, but this November seemed sad and somber. Emil recalled past Novembers as times when he had looked forward to white snow, Chanukah, Christmas. But now I live in fear, thought Emil. And what is worse, I am not alone. We are all frightened. How can it be otherwise? Every day, every night, people are killed, people disappear and we don't know where they are taken. There were rumors that many people were killed just a few kilometers from Brzezany. At this moment, Hesio, a young engineer, entered the pharmacy.

"Good afternoon, Emil."

Emil was happy to see him.

"How are you?" Emil asked.

"I am fine," Hesio said, "but since they took my father, my mother has been very ill. She cannot forgive herself that she didn't go together with him—she doesn't want to live without him."

"Do you have any news about him?"

"No—my father was taken on the street and we didn't hear any more from him. I'm here because I just met Frydzia. She asked me to stop by and pick up some medicine for her child. Little Hela has a high fever."

"Did Frydzia call the doctor?"

"No, the doctor won't come because she lives quite far out. Besides, there is a police station nearby and they stop people very often."

"Don't worry. I have to close the pharmacy in about an hour. I will go myself and bring the medicine for little Hela. At the same time I will see if maybe she needs something special. I can always get it."

Emil said the last words with a twinkle in his eye. When he could help people, he always forgot danger: only the sick person mattered.

Hesio left. Emil filled a small bottle with tablets, took a bottle of alcohol off the shelf. He looked at his watch. It was five minutes to six. He was ready to lock the door when the old man he had been waiting for came in. The man, a lawyer, looked very tired. He was wearing a shabby coat and a woolen scarf. He closed the door and said: "Tomorrow will be a terrible day. There will be a new action and many people will be taken away. I warn you. You had better go home, take your wife and run away."

"But where should I run?" asked Emil.

"You have friends—did they forget you? You have Polish friends and Ukrainian friends. Run, run away."

Emil looked at the old lawyer.

"And what will you do?"

"I?" The lawyer started to laugh. In his laughter there was something frightening.

"I have no place to go, but I am happy because I am ready to be taken away. I want to die. I want to go and argue with Heaven—not with G-d but with Heaven. It must be that the angels have covered the earth and G-d does not see what is going on. I will enter Heaven. I will wrestle with the angels and I will ask G-d to look at the earth—the earth is abandoned, the earth is lonely—G-d cannot see it.''

Emil stared at the old man. He brought him a chair. He went to the back room and came back with a bottle of wine. He poured a little wine into a measuring cup and softly asked the old man to drink.

The old man sat on the chair now and drank. He bent his head down and said: ''Thank you for the wine. I am sure that we see each other for the last time. Please promise me you will flee this city tonight. And don't worry about me. I will see G-d and that is the most important thing.''

''You have time to see G-d,'' said Emil. ''You still have so much to do here—you have your daughter, your grandchildren. They need you—they need a father.''

The old lawyer got up and said: ''I cannot do anything anymore. My son-in-law disappeared. Nobody knows where he is. He was taken with Hesio's father. I believe that my daughter will be stronger when I am not around.''

Emil put his hand on the man's shoulder and softly said:

''Please don't despair. The Lord is One, and the day will come when the angels will uncover His view of the earth and He will come and bring freedom to all of us.''

After the old man left, Emil put his coat on. His shirt was open and as he stepped out the door, the cold wind of November whipped his neck and his throat. He didn't have a scarf, he had given his scarf away to a youngster, the son of a friend. Emil locked up the pharmacy and put up the collar of his coat. The wind blew it down. Under his arm he carried a paper bag with the tablets and alcohol for little Hela. He walked fast. The streets were almost deserted. When he reached the police station a policeman challenged him.

''What are you carrying?''

''Medicine for a patient.''

''Who are you?''

''I am the pharmacist.''

''Open your parcel.'' Emil did so. The policeman took the bottle of tablets.'' They will be good for me,'' he said. ''Now you can go.''

''But I need them,'' Emil said.

The policeman looked at him and said: ''You had better go. Don't argue with a German police officer.''

Emil trudged on. He was sorry that he only had the alcohol to bring for the child. But if she needed something else he could go back to the pharmacy and risk a second journey.

After delivering the alcohol and assuring himself that the child was not seriously ill, Emil went home. His wife and mother-in-law were waiting for him, anxious to know if he'd heard anything new. There were rumors that the next day people would be evacuated—where and when exactly nobody knew. Emil told his wife about the visit of the old lawyer. They both decided to pack a few things, go to Polish friends, ask them to shelter them for the night and help them leave the city at dawn.

"Maybe it will be only for a short time," said Emil.

"Maybe only for a few weeks," said his wife Mila. They both knew they were lying to each other. They looked at their apartment, two small rooms. In the mirror they saw their faces and their faces were already homeless. There was something in the faces that was deeper than sadness—there was the agony of a trapped animal.

For Emil who loved Brzezany so much, this sudden feeling of homelessness was worse than his fear of Germans, worse than anything else. Mila gathered up two dresses, a sweater, some underwear and a pair of shoes.

"You will see," she said, "we will come back."

After packing her things, she took a few of Emil's shirts from the drawer. Emil decided to take very little. He was afraid that if they walked with a big suitcase they could be stopped on the way to their friends. Mila's mother was crying. She didn't want to leave.

"Nobody will take me away—you will see," she said to her daughter. Emil approached her. He talked to her gently. He talked to her exactly as he had talked to the little girl, Hela, an hour ago. With warm and reassuring words he convinced her to go with them.

The old lady insisted on having her silver candlesticks packed.

"I cannot leave them," she said. "I have to light the candles on Friday night. After lighting the candles in these candlesticks for forty-five years, I will not leave them here."

Emil took the candlesticks and packed them carefully in a pink, woolen shawl. He intended to carry them separately.

The old lady took his hand and said:

"Will I ever repay you for your good heart?"

Emil nodded and looked at his watch. It was forbidden for Jews to be on the street after eight o'clock at night.

"Hurry up," he said. "We have only ten minutes left."

They put out the light. First the mother went, then Mila. Emil was the last to leave. He looked around. He wanted to say good-bye to the windows that showed his beloved street every day and to the familiar air, and to the mirror in which he knew he would never again see his face.

# From Kalne to Kozowa

The morning was beautiful, one of those spring mornings in Podolia when the fields are green and the air is so pure and fresh you want to taste it. You open your lips and spring touches your tongue with its sweetness. And there is a fragrance all about, the aroma of jasmine buds on delicate, fragile bushes.

Leon, sitting in a cart pulled by horses, didn't want to think about anything but the loveliness of this morning. He, who had always been a good husband and father to his four children, for perhaps the first time in his life, wanted to forget his responsibilities and contemplate the spring. He felt pain in his chest, a very sharp pain. In the pocket of his vest was the nitroglicerine, which he knew could ease it but he didn't want to move and lose the moment. Besides, it would have been difficult for him to make any movement. He was literally squeezed between his wife Pepcia and his little daughter Adela. Altogether there were seven people in the cart as well as bundles of clothing. Six of the people comprised Leon's family, and the seventh was the driver, a neighbor who had offered to bring the Goldman family to Kozowa.

Leon touched the little hand of Adela. Looking at it, he thought, Adela's skin is like her mother's, very, very fair with a touch of red because of the color of her hair which is also like her mother's. He knew that this color was called Titian brown. Leon had read much about Titian. He was fascinated with the Italian painter, although he had never seen any works of Titian except on postcards. He remembered that when his sister Hania went for her honeymoon to Italy, she had sent him a postcard from Florence with Titian's *Il Venere*. He had treasured the postcard and later, when he met Pepcia, it was always a point in her favor that her hair was the chestnut brown of that painter. Leon looked at Pepcia now. Her long hair was braided and tucked together with a few pins. For a moment, a wave of tenderness passed through his body.

They had married in 1919, immediately after the First World War. The estate of his parents had been devastated during the war, and when the family returned there from Vienna almost nothing was left. His parents built a small house, and after Leon's father died in 1920, Leon built another small house for his family. He was so proud of his four beautiful children. Two boys and two girls. The boys came first, Bunio and Salo, and then the girls, Hanusia and Adela. Adela was named after Leon's sister, who died before the war at the age of sixteen.

Leon's sister had been a beautiful girl, and very talented. Now, on this spring day, jostled in the crowded vehicle, Leon recalled his sister Adela very vividly. She had long, black hair and dark eyes, so unlike the very blue or light green eyes that ran in his family. When Adela fell ill she used to ask to have Ibsen read to her. She loved the Scandinavian author, and she was interested in women's rights. Adela wanted to learn, almost to the last day of her life. Leon's other sister, Lusia, was also very close to Adela. After finishing her lessons with the two governesses (sisters who lived in their parents' home) Lusia would spend long hours with Adela.

In spite of her illness, which was fatal, Adela never lost her hunger for knowledge. Sometimes late at night, Leon would hear Lusia and Adela discussing Plato and Aristotle or practicing their French. They had even read certain forbidden books by de Maupassant and Zola which they had begged the two governesses to lend them. All this in the little village of Podolia, in Kalne. Leon smiled at the thought. It was so good to remember the peaceful times before the First World War.

Still holding the hand of his little daughter, Leon looked at his two sons and his older daughter, Hanusia, who sat opposite him. Hanusia was blonde. She had blue eyes and was very thin. At the moment her eyes were closed; she was asleep. The boys were quiet. Bunio was strong, with a lot of curly, reddish-brown hair, Salo delicate like Hanusia. They were eyeing a field they were passing. Leon followed their stares. The fields, the fields, he thought. These fields have been my whole life. This soil contains my sweat. How many times in his life had he gotten up at dawn, taken his horse and gone into the fields, just to see if they were well cultivated, well fertilized. He fed the fields and the fields fed him and his family. He had loved them always but most of all at harvest time, when people and nature become as one in a beautiful display of harmony.

Leon turned to his children again, his eyes wandering from one face to another.

Bunio is twenty-one years old, Salo seventeen, Hanusia fourteen and Adela eleven. It is like the harvest of my life. In an hour or two or tomorrow, they can be taken away from me. He started to shiver. He didn't know if he was shivering because of his fear or because of his weak heart; nobody noticed fortunately. Silence reigned in the cart. It was moving slowly. In a few minutes they would be out of Kalne, on the big road. The village which was his home was slowly disappearing. He turned his head back, once again, to say goodbye to the fields—he knew it was for good, forever.

Only two days ago he had refused to think about parting from Kalne, but then the order had come for all Jews who lived in the villages thereabout to leave their homes and move to a little town, called Kozowa. Leon now knew why he shivered. It wasn't his heart, it wasn't fear, it was because he was angry. He had never hated anybody, he hadn't known what it meant to hate. His father had implanted in him respect for God and man. But now suddenly he hated the war, he hated the occupier, he hated Nazis. He looked at his two sons and wanted to scream, to tell them: "Get out, run away and kill the enemy." But he could not utter even one word.

When the cart reached the big road, Leon could see many similar carts. German policemen were moving among them, shouting orders. The carts were filled with people and their belongings. The faces of the people looked similar. They were all sad. Even the children were silent.

Leon closed his eyes. He didn't want to see this scene. He preferred his memories. Leon had been born in Brzostek in Western Poland, but when he was a child, his father bought the estate in Podolia and they moved to Kalne. It was a very big estate. Leon's father had bought this estate from a Polish count. There were stables with mirrors because (according to the count) the horses ate better when they saw other horses eating. Leon remembered his arrival in Kalne. He was the oldest and wanted to see everything first. He liked everything he saw and vowed then and there that he would never leave the place. And now he was leaving it forever.

They threw me out, he thought. Who gave them the right? Who gave them the right? In spite of all he had heard and seen, he still believed in justice.

"Leon, Leon," somebody called from the cart passing by. "Where are we going? Do you know if we will have any place to sleep in Kozowa? Leon, you always know everything. Please, answer me." It was Nathan from Krzywe, a friend of Leon's. Nathan's father had been a friend of Leon's father.

"I don't know," answered Leon. "I really don't know." Leon was surprised to hear his voice. He sounded strange, weak and sad. Leon hardly recognized it.

Suddenly he heard a policeman shouting:

"Schnell, schnell (fast, fast)."

The Ukrainian farmer who was driving the Goldmans turned his head to Leon and said: "What do they want from all these people? Is it not enough that they drag them out from their homes?"

"Petro," said Leon, "have you ever seen this kind of treatment?"

"No," said Petro, "I have worked so many years with you, and for you, and you have never said a harsh word to me. My wife said this morning that she will pray for you. You are good people, Mr. Goldman. I remember your mother also—she was a fine, great lady. After her husband died, she took care of everything and she helped us to build the school. She was a good lady."

Petro's head was still turned back when another cart tried to pass by. The two carts collided, and the policeman approached Leon's cart. He told Petro to come down and he hit the peasant with his whip—hard, very hard across the face. When he returned to his place in the cart, a thin stream of blood was flowing from Petro's lips. He wiped the blood with his sleeve.

"I am sorry," said Leon. "I am truly sorry."

"Don't be," answered Petro. "The Germans will be repaid one day. I am right when I say that they are barbarians, although some of my friends like them very much." Petro turned back to Leon again and said, "I am a peasant; I have not learned a lot in my life, but I believe that among people there are good and bad, people who have heart and those who don't. I know good Jews and bad Jews, good Ukrainians and bad Ukrainians; good Poles and bad Poles. Mr. Goldman, I will always remember you."

They were now on the outskirts of Kozowa. It was different here than in the country. There were fewer fields now, and fewer bushes and trees. Small houses became visible. Leon thought about the times when as a young boy, he had come with his father to Kozowa. They would stop in the marketplace, and men would approach his father and ask for advice.

"Mr. Goldman," they used to say, "give us a good advice." Sometimes the advice was simple, sometimes it entailed a loan of money. If a man was poor and didn't have enough for his daughter's wedding, Leon's father would make the necessary arrangements and even buy the trousseau. When somebody was sick and did not have the fee for the doctor, Leon's father took care of it.

Leon looked at Kozowa now. He touched his pocket. He had fifty zlotys—it was everything he possessed. A few days earlier, German policemen, on the pretext of searching his home for weapons, had taken his money and his valuables.

"Pepcia," Leon said to his wife, "you had better take these fifty zlotys from me. It is better that you keep them."

"Why?" asked Pepcia.

"You know, I don't feel well, and I believe you will take better care of them than I do—you always did.'

Leon smiled now, even as he felt the sharp pain in his chest. With his eyes he caressed the Titian hair of his wife, and in the expression of his face was an abundance of love. A minute later he closed his eyes.

Adela took her hand from the hand of her father, and slowly asked her mother, "Why is *Tatus'* (daddy's) hand so cold?"

*In memory of my aunt,*
*Rozia-Ziuta Goldman-Weber*

# Potatoes

Potatoes are important, especially when you are hungry. They are a good source of nourishment; they can take the place of bread. You can cook potatoes in many different ways. If you feel like having soup, you combine potatoes, a lot of water, one carrot, one onion and any other vegetables (if you have them), and you have a tasty broth to warm your whole body. If you feel like having meat and you don't have meat, you can brown one onion (cut in small pieces) in the frying pan (you don't need any grease, just add a little water and mix while frying the onion on a low fire). When the onions are brown you put them into the pot of cooking potatoes. The browned onion gives the potatoes a new flavor, provided that you use only a small amount of water and that you are careful not to burn the mixture. If you are not careful, everything can be ruined. However, if you watch the pot, you will end up with a tasty goulash, a stew without meat.

Rozia looked out the window of her small room and thought about potatoes. Her whole morning was spent thinking about potatoes. In her imagination she saw them light brown, dark brown, small and big, medium size. She even had a place in her room to store them in the corner near the door if she had any.

She glanced at her watch. It was twelve noon. The day was grey and somber, a December day in 1943. A year had passed by since her husband had gone into hiding and she had decided to live as a Christian. She had obtained her Christian paper as a Roman Catholic from her friends who knew a priest. The priest was very helpful. He had saved other people. He had even offered Rozia a room near his church where she could live. At first Rozia thought that it would really be better to leave Lwow, the city in which she had lived for several years, and go to the little village where the priest lived. She even spent a few days in that village, but then she decided to come back to the city. Bertek, her husband, was hidden in Lwow and she couldn't leave him there alone.

Her husband was unable to live in the open as a non-Jew, he was afraid that his dark hair and black eyes would betray him. He kept saying: ''I look Jewish, I cannot play games.'' Rozia could pass for an Aryan. She had green eyes, light brown hair, a very Slavic round face. "You look like ten Christians, not like one—nobody will suspect that you are Jewish," Bertek said, and he was right.

During the past year she often walked alone on the street. Sometimes she travelled to the country for food and nobody suspected she was Jewish. Men would flirt with her, try to make her acquaintance. She knew she was good looking. She was petite, feminine, and from her childhood on, people had called her "a beautiful Rozia."

Whenever she had accompanied her mother on their summer vacations, they used to say: "You are a good-looking woman, Mrs. Goldman, but where did you get this beauty?" Her mother had one answer only: "My daughter Rozia looks like her father."

Rozia remembered her father well, although he had died when she was fifteen, right after the First World War, in 1920. During the war she saw him very little. He spent four years in the Austrian Army, serving as an officer with his older son, Mulo. Rozia spent the war years together with her mother, her brothers who were not of age to serve in the army, and her sisters, in Vienna. Rozia remembered that after the war, when they came home to the estate, Kalne was in ruins. Her father looked at the place where their beautiful home had stood and said: "Don't worry, we will build another home again."

This home built in the year of their return was not as big or as beautiful as their former one, but it was a home.

In 1920 fighting was still going on in certain parts of Poland and many fugitives passed through their village. One night a young woman came to the Goldman estate and asked for shelter. There were already other people in Rozia's parents' home, and the estate superintendent told the woman that there was no place for her. Rozia's father happened to be passing by. He told the woman she could stay, assuring her that there was room in his house for one person more.

During the night the young woman became very ill. She had typhoid. Rozia's father, her older sister, and Rozia herself contracted the disease. The young woman, Rozia and her older sister survived but not her father.

When Rozia's father died it seemed to Rozia that the whole world had collapsed. Rozia was distraught. If it had not been for her older sister Lusia, Rozia might never have come back to herself, especially after her long illness. Lusia, the tiny, thin sister had taken care of all of them, Rozia's father, her older sister, the young woman stranger and Rozia during the typhoid. Lusia had not been afraid that she would catch the contagious disease. She nursed everybody for several weeks. And then she continued to care for Rozia through the depression that followed her recovery.

But Lusia had always been remarkable. During the war, it was she who had brought up the younger brothers and sisters. She was bright, energetic and loved to go out. She was always hurrying off to the opera and theater. But after coming home late at night, she would mend the torn socks of her brothers, sew clothes for her sisters and rise early the next day to teach the youngsters history, literature and her favorite subject, philosophy.

If I were more of a philosopher, Rozia thought, maybe I could manage my life better.

But her thoughts kept coming back to potatoes. She opened a little drawer and she took out a piece of paper, a food ration coupon entitling her to buy a bag of potatoes. In her mind she could see the store where the potatoes were sold. It was on a street not far from the hospital where she had worked as a nurse.

Originally Rozia had wanted to study medicine, but nobody in the family seemed to understand her ambition. When her sister Lusia married in 1921 Rozia was really alone. After the death of her father Rozia's mother was very busy with the estate. She had to provide bread for her young children, and Rozia was forced to take care of herself. For a few years after finishing high school, Rozia helped her mother manage the estate. She had given up her dream of becoming a doctor and couldn't think of getting married because she still had one older single sister, Ginia. According to family rules, this older sister had to marry before Rozia could. Once a year Rozia visited her two married sisters, Hania and Lusia, who already had children, and once a year she vacationed with her mother in Czechoslovakia. There in Marienbad or Karlsbad, she tasted the luxury and pleasure of being with people, who came from different parts of Europe. At the same time she thought of her future. On one of their vacation trips she told her mother that she wanted to leave the estate and become a nurse. It was difficult for Rozia's mother to understand the desire of her daughter but, finally, Rozia won. She left the house and became a nurse in the hospital. Her older sister still had not married and while Rozia was waiting, her work was her main joy in life.

At the beginning of the Second World War Rozia had married. Bertek Weber, a lawyer, was a very warm-hearted, intelligent man. Rozia loved him very much. They lived in a small apartment and they were very happy. Rozia remembered now how important every evening was to her. For years she had longed for love. She knew that she could have had many lovers, but she had decided to wait, to have only one, her husband. Somehow she thought that this way she would continue to be more herself. When she married, Bertek gave her all the affection she could have hoped for. He was full of love. Bertek was rather short and skinny with a very expressive face. He talked fast, he was always too busy, except for bringing and giving love. For that he had all the time in the world. Rozia was amazed and charmed by this quality of his. It was then that Bertek began calling her Ziuta instead of Rozia because he thought that Ziuta was a softer name.

During most of the first two years of their marriage, Lwow was occupied by the Russians. Conditions were difficult but Bertek managed to bring her anything she needed. When the Germans came and the situation became more difficult, Rozia and Bertek at first still had their happy moments each evening in their apartment.

As the situation became more and more dangerous, their times in bed became most precious. Encircled by her husband's arms, feeling his warm body every inch of which belonged to her (she knew), Rozia-Ziuta could renew her hopes and reject the ill logic of the war. She could be grateful to God and to destiny that she was loved. To be loved is the greatest gift of life, she thought. Because of that love, Rozia didn't want to leave Lwow, even though she too rarely saw Bertek.

It was a Polish family that provided him shelter, a very small room in the back of an apartment. Bertek was paying well, she knew, but lately the family had contacted Rozia and demanded more money. She was sure Bertek didn't know about this but Rozia, anxious that her husband be well treated, had given the family almost all the money she possessed. She was left with a few hundred zlotys and a small diamond ring. The reason that she wanted the bag of potatoes was that it could provide her food for the next several weeks. Again she thought about the color and the sizes of potatoes. If she had the bag of potatoes, she could give the rest of her money to the Polish family when they demanded more, as she was sure they would. She knew that if she did not get the potatoes, she would have to use that money to buy food and even potatoes were quite expensive if not bought with a coupon. She was proud that she had obtained the ration coupon for the potatoes. It had been quite dangerous to get it with her forged documents, but she had accomplished the task.

The time was flying. Should I go or not? she asked herself. What if somebody recognizes me near the grocery store? She had passed the place often, years before, going to the hospital. She wished she had somebody to ask for advice, but she didn't have anyone. She was renting a little room in the apartment of an older Polish woman who worked long hours every day. The woman was pleasant. She liked Rozia and of course didn't suspect that Rozia was Jewish. She rented her the room because Rozia had been recommended to her by the Polish friend who had provided the false documents.

If she knew I am Jewish she would certainly put me out of her apartment in an hour, Rozia thought. Oh, I can't blame her. It takes a lot of courage to help Jews today. She suddenly realized that she had thought about Jews apart from herself. She had gotten so used to the idea that she was Aryan, Catholic, a role she had been playing for a year, that she sometimes believed it. Except for her husband, whom she saw once every two weeks, she had not met any Jews for seven or eight months.

Yes, Rozia decided, she would go for the potatoes. She dressed herself. She got out the nice brown coat that Bertek had bought her during the Russian occupation. It was warm with a fur collar. All the Jews had had to give up their furs in the first year of the German occupation, but Bertek had insisted that she keep this coat. Bertek was right. The small fur collar, touching her face, so that she could breathe it, provided her with warmth even on the coldest day.

On the street, Rozia looked back. It was a habit to assure herself that no one was following her. She took the tram; the grocery store was far away. While sitting in the tram which she had used to take to the hospital, Rozia thought about the time she had been a nurse. She had loved best working in the psychiatric wing. She had a lot of patience and compassion for the patients. It was true, she thought, that mental patients could be difficult but they were people, the unhappy people, who lived in their own worlds, so different from the world of ordinary folk. Rozia often thought that her patients needed love, and that if they would be surrounded with love, they might be brought back to "normalcy." She remembered discussing this idea with a prominent psychiatrist. The psychiatrist told her that, indeed, some people lose their way because they are lonely too long, and it was possible that these could be strengthened with more love and understanding. But the majority of Rozia's colleagues remained skeptical. They called her "the incurable optimist who thinks that love is the best remedy for all sicknesses in the world."

The tram stopped. Rozia got out. There was a long line before the store. Rozia got to the end of the line. There were at least a hundred people before her. She tried to hide her face in the little fur collar. She felt uncomfortable. She was trembling. She was afraid. I did wrong, she thought, to come here. It is too near the hospital. Somebody could recognize me. Somebody who is not friendly. Although she didn't know of any enemies she had in the hospital, she knew that anti-Semitic feeling was strong in Poland. Poles did not like Germans, but some of them didn't like Jews even more.

Rozia felt a hand on her shoulder. She turned her head. A nurse whom she knew from the hospital stood near her.

"What are you doing here?" asked the nurse.

"I am waiting for my ration of potatoes," Rozia said.

"And who gave you the right to get these potatoes? These potatoes are not for Jews." Now the nurse raised her voice. "Look at her—she is Jewish—she pretends that she is not. We have had enough of Jews."

"Leave her alone," said a man standing ahead of Rozia.

"Leave her alone," said a woman. "She didn't do anything wrong."

"Why should I leave her alone? She is Jewish. Let her go where she belongs."

The nurse turned to a Polish policeman who stood nearby.

"Take her to the police station. She is Jewish."

The policeman approached Rozia.

"Are you Jewish?" he asked.

The policeman had a kind face.

Rozia said: "No, I am not Jewish."

"But she is," insisted the nurse, "and I am demanding you to take her in."

The policeman tried to calm the nurse, but she persisted. At last the policeman said to Rozia "Come with me."

Rozia was now walking with the policeman. She thought that she might bribe him with the small diamond ring that she had on her finger.

"Let me go," she said in a pleading voice.

"We will see," said the policeman.

They turned the corner of the street, and at that moment the nurse appeared running.

"I want to see this woman at the police station," she said. "I will assist you."

A few hours later Rozia was in prison, the worst prison in Lwow called *Brigitki*. In a well-decorated room in which a picture of Hitler hung on the wall, a Gestapo man asked her with a smile. "A beautiful Jewish woman wanted to pass as Christian? You could have. But we know that you are Jewish. Admit that you are Jewish. Admit!"

The smile vanished and he hit Rozia's face. Hard, very hard.

In a moment Rozia became dizzy and around her she saw, as before in her room, only potatoes. They were brown, small, big, and of medium size. The potatoes are important when you are hungry, she thought.

*In memory of my uncle,*
*Benio Goldman*

# The Woodcutter

B enio held an axe in his hand. The wood of the handle was cold. Benio tried
not to change the position of his hand while hacking the branches of a tree
lying on the ground, because as long as his hand held the handle of the axe in one
place it retained some warmth. The night was very cold. January is always cold
here, Benio thought, and he continued his work, trying not to think. No—he
didn't want to think. It was better to concentrate on cutting the wood which
would afterwards provide some warmth in the hut where he lived with his
fiancée, Gusta.

The hut had served, many years ago, as a shelter for shepherds in summer. It
was good for summer, a place to hide from a storm, but not for January. He
became very irritated. He was thinking again. He knew that if he dwelt too much
in his mind, he would not survive, and he wanted to survive—it was that simple.
He could not believe that Hitler would win the war. Impossible. And in spite of
the indifference of the world to the suffering, Benio thought that the Americans
would do something sooner or later. The Americans would bring an end to the
suffering. Yes, Benio had hope, he always had. At school he had been a poor
student. He hadn't liked to study. Before exams in high school he used to tell his
mother: "I hope, I hope that I will make it."

He was a very good-looking boy and, later, a very good-looking man. He
was strong like a bull, people used to say. He was quite tall, broad-shouldered
with green eyes and black hair. Though he had no head for study, he was
interested in agriculture. He was also interested in women. He loved them
both—the women and the soil. Since boyhood his favorite sports had been riding
horses and chasing after girls. Thus he acquired great physical strength; at the age
of eighteen his eyes began to go bad. The doctors said they had no cure for him.
One of them told him that medicine was progressing, that in a few years a new
technique of surgery might be developed which could correct his condition.
When Benio heard this man's opinion, he said to himself, "I am young, I will
wait, I hope . . ."

At the beginning of the war Benio was thirty-two years old. He was engaged to Gusta. He intended to marry her in October 1939 but with the coming of the war the marriage was postponed. Instead Benio moved into Gusta's parents' house. He didn't have his own apartment, because he had always lived in the country, in Kalne, on his mother's very big estate. He worked there with his mother and his older brother Leon. They were the only ones who had remained on the estate. His other brothers and sisters were already married or lived and worked in the city. The older brother, Samuel (Mulo), was a medical doctor, a specialist in dermatology; another, Emil, was a pharmacist; his four sisters lived in different places.

Benio adored the country. It gave him great satisfaction to supervise the people working in the fields. He had a lot of compassion for the peasants and they liked him. Even when he saw that the work was not well done, he was never harsh; he was always able to correct things with a kind word and a smile.

Benio put the axe on the ground. With a sleeve he wiped his forehead. In spite of the frost, he was sweating freely. He looked at his watch. It was six o'clock in the morning. He was happy that the moon was shining and the sky had many stars. Without their light he knew he would not be able to work. His eyes were much worse than before. It must be because he was not being nourished properly. The doctors had said that he needed a lot of protein. He laughed at this thought. He was happy that he and Gusta had a few potatoes to eat, a piece of bread, and some beans or turnips every day. Since they had come to live in the forest, far away from the village, Yvan, one of the peasants who had worked for many years on the estate, brought vegetables, bread and milk to them twice weekly. Near the hut was a well, and they could have water at least any time. Gusta boiled water several times a day and they drank this with a bit of milk. They had come to like this beverage. Altogether they were used to their food now. Benio was sorry only that Gusta had lost a lot of weight. She had always been rather thin, but now she was only skin and bones.

Gusta and Benio had come to the hut following "the last action" in Brzezany, where they lived. This "action" had claimed the lives of many, many Jews. The Gestapo had surrounded the ghetto at night and in the morning two thousand people had vanished. Nobody knew where. It was a miracle that Benio and Gusta were not taken. Because they had been hidden in a cave by Ukrainian friends, they were saved. In the afternoon Benio and Gusta went back to Gusta's parents' apartment. Her parents as well as her sister were gone.

When they realized that they were alone, alone of all their family, they did not know what to do. They went back to the Ukrainian friends and asked them to contact Yvan in Kalne. Benio believed that this faithful worker and friend would find a place for them to hide. He was right. Late in the evening Yvan came to Brzezany. It was dangerous for him to help his Jewish friend but he agreed to take care of Benio and Gusta. Benio and Gusta packed a few things, then Benio gave Yvan his money and said: "I trust you like my own brother. We are putting our lives in your hands."

Gusta and Benio had tears in their eyes when they left the city. Yvan told them that they would see Brzezany again. Then he brought them to the hut. He said that since the Goldman family had left the estate which was taken first by Russians in November 1939, and later by Germans in June 1941, no one ever used this primitive shelter.

"Not only is it not used," Yvan said, "but people never pass this place."

For Benio and Gusta it seemed ideal in the beginning, but when the frost came and the wind started to blow through the window, the situation became difficult. However, the hut contained an old stove. At the forest, first Benio collected the fallen branches. Later he asked Yvan to lend him the axe.

Since Benio had gotten the axe, everything had changed. He was able to have as much wood as he wanted and the hut became "quite a home," as Gusta put it one day. But while they had heat enough, they began to worry about running out of light. Their supply of kerosene was dwindling and kerosene was difficult to come by these days. The kerosene lamp was very important to Benio and Gusta. The nights were long, and as long as they had light they could read. They had brought a few books with them. The one they loved best was *Pan Tadeusz* by Adam Mickiewicz. There were long parts of *Pan Tadeusz* that Benio knew by heart. He was not a good student but he loved poetry. Mickiewicz was his idol.

"How is it that Mickiewicz understood Jews better than other Poles?" Benio asked Gusta. "Mickiewicz knew that many Jews loved Poland deeply and sacrificed their lives for her." There was one part of *Pan Tadeusz* which was called "Jankiel's Concert," in which a Jewish country musician plays on his dulcimer a song of love for Poland and Poland's freedom. In "Jankiel's Concert," Mickiewicz conveyed the deep sense of Jews of belonging to the soil on which they lived.

Thinking about Mickiewicz and Jews, Benio stopped working. The Jews, the Jews, where are they now? he wondered. Some in the camps, some in the ghettos, surrounded by killers or bystanders. How many bystanders are like my good Yvan? He was so grateful to Yvan for taking care of him and Gusta. It was true that before the war he had always helped. He had helped with money when Yvan wanted to make his home larger or when one of Yvan's sons wanted to go to high school in the city. Benio never considered that one day he would need Yvan's help. And he trusted Yvan but Gusta did not. In recent weeks they had quarrelled about Yvan. Gusta did not mistrust Yvan on his own account but because of his brother, Stepan.

"Stepan is dangerous," Gusta had said, "and one day, if Stepan finds out that we are here, Yvan will not be able to save us." Benio thought that Gusta was worrying too much.

"That's enough for this morning." The voice of Gusta came from the threshhold of the hut.

"Please come, my woodcutter."

Benio entered the hut with a lot of wood in his arms. Gusta helped him bring the wood to the stove. Gusta was small. She had long blond hair braided at the top of her head. The kerosene lamp lit up her face and Benio saw the sad eyes. They were ordinarily a pale blue, but in the light of the lamp seemed paler than usual.

Suddenly it occurred to Benio that in her long blue housecoat, Gusta looked almost like a child, a sickly child. He touched her forehead.

"Gusta, are you ill?"

"Oh, no," said Gusta stepping back. "I am fine." She tried to smile. "I am well. And how is my strong woodcutter?" She moved toward Benio, kissed him once, twice.

Benio didn't know why, but for the first time since they had come to the hut, he was afraid. He didn't know if it was because Gusta was so very pale or because the sound of the wind had brought him an awareness of their vulnerability. Gusta took Benio's hands in her hands. He looked at them, so white, delicate.

"Your hands are beautiful," he said.

Gusta laughed. "And your hands," she said, "are the hands of a woodcutter. Thanks to these hands we can enjoy our stove."

"Oh, now," said Benio, "not only because of my hands—this axe," he pointed, "helps us beyond any expectation. I am very grateful to Yvan that he gave this axe to us."

"What can the woodcutter talk about?" said Gusta. "Naturally about his axe."

They both laughed now. The wind had stopped and Benio's fear passed. Day was breaking and Gusta looked better in the morning light.

They sat down to breakfast. They ate bread and drank water with milk. Gusta washed the two cups and two plates in a little basin and put them aside on the table. Then they looked out the window. Near the edge of the forest stood two men.

"Who can they be?" asked Benio. He knew that Gusta could not answer.

Slowly the two men were approaching the hut.

"What should we do?" asked Gusta.

"Nothing," answered Benio. "Let's wait."

"For what?" said Gusta.

"I don't know," answered Benio. He was not afraid now. What would be would be. If one of these two men was not Yvan, Benio knew that they were lost. The two men came closer.

"One of them is Yvan," said Benio.

Gusta made a quick movement. She took her big woolen shawl and said: "I am going out. I don't want to wait here."

Without a word and before Benio could say something, she opened the door and ran toward the bushes behind the hut. Even though it was winter, the bushes were dense. Benio did not follow her. He continued watching at the window. The two men passed the hut. They didn't even stop at the door. However, they stopped near the bushes and discussed something in very loud voices. A few minutes later they left. Benio watched until he lost them in the fields. He went out to the bushes and found Gusta.

Gusta was trembling. Her eyes were in tears. Benio took her gently in his arms like a child and brought her home.

"Why are you crying?" Benio asked, when they were again inside the hut.

For a little while Gusta could not talk. She lay on the straw mattress. Her lips were violet. She looked like a trapped animal.

"Please talk," said Benio softly. There was something in Gusta's eyes that Benio had never seen before. Not sadness but apathy, as if the world around her did not exist any more.

At last she said: "I heard them. Yvan came with his brother. Stepan said that the time had come to finish the Jews. He said Yvan should think of his family rather than of the damn Jews, especially these Jews who don't have any more money.

"Get rid of them," Stepan said. "They gave you everything they had. You can use their money for something important. It is so cold now and you have to come here all the time to bring them something to eat. Don't care for the Jews. If you want to care for somebody care for your brother, not those, the damn Jews."

Gusta stopped at this point and again Benio saw that terrible look. And Gusta was trembling again. Benio boiled some water. He covered Gusta with every cover they had, with every coat, but she continued to shake. He tried to make her drink some hot water with milk. She could not. He took a spoon and forced some of the liquid into Gusta's mouth. She didn't swallow. Benio lay down with her on the straw mattress and tried to warm Gusta with his body. She was trembling, trembling. At last she fell asleep. He listened to her breathing. She was breathing heavily, but she had stopped trembling. For a moment Benio forgot the danger, Yvan, Stepan. He was glad that Gusta was resting.

Benio got up. He approached the window. Black patches of vegetation stood out on the frozen ground like the squares of a chessboard. Chess, he thought. He had liked to play chess. He had even taught his youngest nephew, Adam, Lusia's son, how to play. The boy will never forget that I taught him this fascinating game. But will Adam, my nephew, really remember me? After—after what? Benio asked himself. He didn't want to finish the thought. Again he looked through the window. The world looks like a chessboard and I am in a chess match. Have I lost the game? I who was a winner so many times even against adversaries who were very strong. *But you didn't play Hitler*, an inner voice said. *You didn't play Hitler*, the voice repeated.

Benio decided not to think for a while but rather to do something constructive. He went to the stove and put more wood in it. But he could not refrain from thinking. He thought of what Gusta had told him and suddenly like lightning, an idea came to him.

Gusta was sick. She could not have heard what Stepan or Yvan was saying.

Whatever Gusta had heard was the work of her imagination. She must be very sick. He had to do something for her. He still had a few of the pills which his brother, the pharmacist, had given him when they had lived together in Brzezany. Benio knew that Gusta had a special place for them. Where could they be? He looked around. If he could find the aspirin, Benio thought, Gusta might be better in a few hours. At last he found it in Gusta's purse, four white tablets. Benio knew that Gusta could not easily swallow them whole. He took two of the pills, crushed them on a spoon and woke up Gusta. He begged her to take the medicine. For a moment she seemed to be better. She swallowed, drank some water and almost immediately fell back asleep. Her breathing was not as heavy as before.

It was four o'clock in the afternoon. The January day was coming to the end. Benio decided to boil some potatoes. He peeled the potatoes very carefully. He didn't want to lose even a gram of the white with the skins. He hated potato skin; even in these bad times with food scarce, he couldn't bring himself to eat it. He looked at Gusta. She seemed to be better. Some color had returned to her face. He put the potatoes on the stove, covered the pot. His mother had always said that potatoes cook better and faster when they are covered. He thought of his mother. She had been tall and strong, stronger than he was now.

He sat in darkness listening to the water boil. He didn't light the kerosene lamp. He decided to light it only when Gusta was better. The axe was near the door. He wanted to go out and cut some more wood, but he was afraid to leave Gusta alone.

Suddenly the door flew open. Benio was blinded for a moment by a powerful flashlight. He closed his eyes. When he opened them again he saw Yvan and Stepan. Yvan was holding the flashlight. Stepan picked up the axe which lay near the door and ran towards Benio.

*In memory of my aunt,*
*Ginia Goldman*

# The Narrow Bed

The room in which Ginia lived was quite large. On one side, near the wall, stood a square table and four chairs. In a corner was a gas stove with two burners, and beside it a wood stove which was afire all winter, because the room was cold. Near the door were two twin beds put together and covered with an embroidered bedspread. The bedspread looked strange in this room, like a reminder of another, better world. Near the joined twin beds was a crib, which was really a big basket on wheels. A baby was asleep in it.

In the corner of the room, opposite the stoves, was a narrow wooden bed. This bed looked like a little mountain of four pillows and a quilt filled with down. This bed was not made. A suitcase showed from under it. The suitcase bulged; it contained all of Ginia's portable belongings except for the embroidered spread, which she had given to the people with whom she shared the room. Ginia had lived in this place for a month. Before that she had lived elsewhere with another family. With them she had had her own room. However, one day the German authorities had issued an order for all Jews to live only in one area and Ginia had had to move. She took with her her bed and the suitcase. She was very glad to have her own bed. Her Polish neighbor, Janek Opole, transported the bed in his cart pulled by two horses. Ginia was grateful to Janek Opole. It had been his idea to bring the bed here.

"You will feel better, Miss Ginia, if you at least have your own bed," he said.

Janek had been right. This bed—it was a little like having one's own home, thought Ginia. She especially liked her eiderdown. Even when the room was very cold, she was warm as long as she stayed in her bed covered with her quilt.

Ginia was kneeling. She was wearing dark brown stockings and a pair of very shabby shoes. It was because of the latter that she was trying to find a pair of sneakers in her suitcase. She was sure that she had had the sneakers when she came to this apartment, and she decided to wear them now. She planned to go to a shoemaker and have the shoes repaired because they really had become impossible. There was a hole in the front of the left shoe and another in the back. If she found the sneakers, she could wear them until the shoes were mended. She had a few zlotys which she had saved for "a dark hour," as she always called an emergency, and she would spend part of this money now. The shoes must be repaired, she had decided. She had not found the sneakers yet but while tossing through the various contents of the suitcase, underwear, bedding, two table-cloths, she came upon an envelope. The envelope contained a few snapshots. Ginia slowly looked at them, one by one. She stopped at a picture of a young man. She held the picture in her hand and her eyes wandered from the eyes of the young man to his lips. I really loved him, Ginia thought. I wanted so much to marry him. Ginia had always hungered for love, but somehow it was always passing by, never stopping for long near her.

There hadn't been much luck in her life. She often felt pushed by everybody and everything. Even in her family circumstances were hard for her. Why, wondered Ginia, had she had a more difficult life than her brothers and sisters? Maybe it was because she had been a bit slower than they were and not as good looking. She nevertheless resented the fact. Except for her older sister, Lusia, nobody seemed to care, especially after she lost her father in 1920, when she was seventeen. There was always somebody in the family who didn't get along with her, and therefore she often felt lonely and miserable.

She knew that she was jealous. Her younger sister, Rozia, was very beautiful and people would say: "Look at them—two sisters and so different." If Rozia were not Ginia's sister, Ginia would not have seemed so plain. Ginia knew that she was not a beauty, but she was not ugly. When she was far away from Rozia, she was confident and able to make friends.

Some of them assured her that even if she was not conventionally pretty, there was something special about her that was more than beauty. One of her friends, Milek, told her once: "You make me think of a fairy with your green eyes, dark skin and slender body and when you laugh it reminds me of chimes ringing." Ginia never forgot these words, although she hadn't laughed in a long time.

Ginia looked again at the picture of the young man.

"Why didn't you marry me?" she asked aloud. She asked this question a million times. "I loved you so much. Maybe if we had married I would today have a child with your eyes and your lips." Ginia put the pictures back in the envelope. She put the envelope carefully back in the suitcase as if she were hiding a treasure. It was a treasure for her. The envelope contained not just pictures, but the one and only love in her life, and her unforgotten dreams.

Somebody entered the room. It was Eva, the mother of the baby. Eva was very young. Her blond hair was in disorder. Ginia got up. She left her suitcase open. She forgot that she had been searching for her sneakers. Eva looked scared. She began to cry.

"What happened?" asked Ginia.

"I went to the prison," Eva said. "Bolek is there no more. Nobody knows where he was taken. I don't want to live any more in this world, where every crime is permitted. Ginia, promise me you will take care of the baby. I want to look for my husband. I love him. Do you understand? No, you will not understand, because you have never been married. You don't know what it is to feel a man's body as if it were your own. You don't know what it means to see the world through your husband's eyes, you don't know!'' She was weeping.

Ginia looked at Eva. She didn't utter a word. She had been hurt to the quick, but it didn't matter. She was used to being hurt. The important thing was to bring Eva to her senses.

"Don't cry," Ginia said, "you will see—after a day or two Bolek will come back. He is young and strong, and he always finds his way home. Remember, two weeks ago he escaped from the police station and came home.''

"Yes, but this time it was not a police station. He was in prison, and today the Gestapo took all the prisoners to an undisclosed place.''

Ginia tried to put her arms around Eva. It was difficult; Ginia's arms were short and skinny and Eva was big. The top of Ginia's head barely reached Eva's chin. Eva was the image of a sensual woman. Every part of her body was rounded, reminding of her sex. She was perhaps a little too heavy but even her heaviness seemed to accentuate her femininity. Fumbling, Ginia tried to calm her. She told Eva that she must be strong for the baby, that wherever Bolek was now, he would wish that Eva did not forget that besides being a wife she was also a mother.

Eva stopped crying for a moment. She walked to the crib. The baby was now awake. The little infant boy looked at his mother with immense blue eyes. He tried to sit up but he was not strong enough.

"Look at him," said Eva." He is one year old and he cannot sit without help. He is weak because my milk is not rich enough and I cannot feed him properly.''

"What will I do?'' Eva started to cry again.

At last she calmed down and took little Henio from his crib. She opened her dress and started to nurse the baby. The little boy licked the nipple of his mother's breast and slowly started to suck. After a while he stopped.

"Why are you not drinking?'' asked Eva. The baby looked up at her and started to cry.

"You see? This is the answer. I don't have milk anymore.'' She squeezed her nipple hard. Not a drop came from it.

Eva buttoned her dress. She put the child into the crib and said to Ginia. "I am going to the corner, I will beg the owner of the store to give me a bottle of milk.''

"Take this,'' said Ginia. She handed Eva a few zlotys, the money that she had intended to use to have her shoes repaired.

"Take this and buy not only milk, but try to get some cereal or potatoes.

That storekeeper gets everything on the black market. Go and get food for your child.''

Eva obeyed. She opened the door and Ginia heard her steps descending the staircase. The baby started to cry again. Ginia went to the gas stove, boiled some water and mixed in a cup with a quarter of a spoon of honey. She had gotten the honey from Janek Opole, the man who had brought her bed to this apartment. She poured the mixture into a baby bottle. She took the baby in her arms, pressed him against her breast. "I am sorry," she said to the baby." I don't have a breast like your mother, I don't have milk but I will try to feed you with honey—honey is good." The child drank, at first slowly, then he began to gulp. "Thank God that you like honey," Ginia said.

With the child in her hands she walked to the window. Below on the street she saw many people running in different directions. Why? she asked herself. Why? Where are they running?

At the corner near the grocery store, Ginia saw Eva. She was entering the store. Ginia wished that Eva had not gone out. If people are running, something is wrong.

The baby stopped drinking. There was still some water and honey in the bottle, and Ginia thought that it would be better if the baby finished it. She forced the rubber nipple into the infant's mouth but the little boy refused it. She knew that the baby has to burp before being returned to bed. She patted his back several times till he made a small noise. I would have been a good mother, Ginia thought.

She pressed the little boy to her breast. It was so good to feel the baby against her. She decided to change his diapers. In the kettle was still a little warm water. She took a towel. She wet it and washed the baby, his whole body. He needed it. Eva hadn't given him a bath in two days.

"I want you to be clean," she whispered in the child's ear. After changing the baby, Ginia felt better. She put the baby in the crib, but the little boy was unhappy. He screamed; he wouldn't become quiet. "You need company," said Ginia.

She took him in her arms and went to the window. The street was very noisy. Opposite the house a truck stopped. The truck was full of Gestapo men. The men all got out except for the driver. In a minute or two some of the Gestapo men began entering houses.

Then Ginia saw Eva leaving the store. She was holding a big brown bag. A Gestapo man approached her. He took the brown bag from her hands. Eva started to remonstrate with him. She tried to grab the bag. Another Gestapo man joined them. From behind he pushed Eva toward the truck, then forced her into it. Ginia didn't want to see any more. She took the baby, grabbed the bottle with the remaining water and honey and, without thinking, opened the door. She left the door of the room wide open and as fast as she could raced down the steps. She passed the front door and ran to the basement. In it was a cavern without any door, but she could get into it through a hole in the wall. Slowly and carefully, she approached the cavern. A ray of light came from a window opposite it. She held the child tight, climbed through the hole, and sat down on the floor of soft earth and small stones. She was now in complete darkness. The child was sleeping. Far away she heard people crying and men shouting. She didn't know how long she sat in the darkness. Once she got up with the child in her arms and peered through the hole in the wall to see if it was still daylight. She was afraid to leave. The whole house seemed to be deserted. Everybody had gone or been taken. Ginia fell asleep with the infant in her arms, its bottle in her hand.

She didn't know how long she had slept; she only knew that it was time to get up and give the baby something to eat. Carefully feeling her way she climbed through the hole again. Through the little window she looked at the sky. It was night now. She saw two stars in the sky. Suddenly a childish thought came to her. You'd better take care of me, she told the stars silently. When she was a child and nobody wanted to play with her at night when she could not sleep, she had talked thus to the stars. They became her friends.

Ginia went upstairs. The house was empty. She knew that she was alone in it. What happened to all my neighbours? Ginia thought. However, she had a more immediate problem to deal with; she had to change the baby. He was soaking wet.

She entered the apartment and put some water on the burner. When the water was lukewarm, Ginia washed the baby and put him into his crib. She didn't know what to give him to eat. In a little pantry was a slice of bread. Ginia boiled some water, broke the bread into little pieces and soaked them in the water; then she mixed in a half spoon of honey. She took the baby from his crib, sat down near the table and slowly started to feed the baby with a spoon. I must be careful, Ginia thought. God forbid, he can choke. However, the baby didn't give her any trouble. He ate well.

When he had finished, Ginia prepared the bottle of water with honey and the baby drank almost the whole bottle.

"Henio, you are a man," Ginia said. She put the baby into his crib. She ate the remaining bread and an apple. She drank some hot water. She looked for the diapers. There were only five. She decided to wash now. I will need them, she thought. She boiled the diapers as Eva used to do in a basin on the stove. She rinsed them and hung them on the string near the window to dry.

The baby was sleeping now. Ginia washed herself in the same basin in which she had boiled the diapers. She always tried to keep clean. She was happy that she had another four pieces of soap. I am rich, she thought. Five pieces of soap is a lot these days. She tried to push away her thoughts. She approached her bed. The open suitcase stared at her, its contents in complete disorder. My whole life looks like this suitcase, Ginia thought.

She undressed herself. Now, in her nightgown, she felt the chill of the room. In March the weather should be nicer. Everything is upside down. Even spring does not want to come here.

She tried to think about everything except Eva. Now she had to think only of Henio, the little innocent being asleep in the crib. She realized that all the time she had been in the room the light was on. Maybe I made a mistake, she thought. If really no one lives in this house anymore, the light should be out. However, she did not turn it off. She looked at her nightgown. It was white and near the neckline a few roses were embroidered. Many times Ginia had hoped this gown would serve her on her wedding night. It was part of a trousseau her mother had prepared and Ginia had never used. The embroidered spread she had given to Eva and Bolek was also a part of that trousseau. The couple had had simply nothing to cover their bed. Eva had said that after the war, when Ginia was married, she would buy a new bedspread, a beautiful one, for Ginia and her husband.

Ginia walked to her own bed. It is comfortable, she thought. She lay now under the cover, her head resting on two pillows. She had placed the other two besides her on a chair. She touched the quilt—it was silky and soft. She enjoyed the silk between her fingers. She pushed her hair away from her face. Her hair was silky. She knew she had nice hair, light brown and soft, it was her best feature. Ginia closed her eyes but she could not sleep. Although she knew that it would be better to turn off the light and lie in darkness, she hesitated to do so. She thought the darkness would frighten her.

However, after a long while, she got out of bed. Before turning off the light she took the baby from his crib. She held Henio in her arms. He was cold.

I won't let you freeze, precious one, she thought. She took the baby to her bed. She covered him with the quilt, and she turned off the light. She didn't want to think about the morrow.

Now, lying in her bed, she felt the baby's body pressing against her breast. She put her arms around him. This bed is narrow, thought Ginia. I never knew that this bed was so narrow.

*To my aunt,*
*Lunia Birman-Goldman and*
*Gizela-Dzidzia Goldman,*
*the daughter of*
*Lunia and Dr. Samuel Goldman*

# Brahms' Lullaby

L unia and Dzidzia were among the many people who arrived at Auschwitz that evening. The Goldman family—the father, Dr. Samuel Goldman, the mother, Lunia, and their daughter, Dzidzia, were brought there from Tarnow, the city where they lived, in a long train. Dzidzia held her father's hand. She was nine and a half years old, was tall and she looked older. Dzidzia resembled her mother. She had dark eyes and dark hair. She didn't look at all like her father who was a short man with a very fair complexion, light green eyes and brown wavy hair.

Dzidzia's father was short, but he was strong. She could feel his strength in his fingers with which from time to time he squeezed her own.

Dzidzia looked up at her mother who walked beside them. Dzidzia's mother was tall, taller than Dzidzia's father. Each of the Goldmans carried a small suitcase. Dzidzia was tired and sleepy. She was more tired and sleepy than afraid.

She held the hand of her father and wished that this trip were a dream and that she could go back to her room in Tarnow. She heard a child crying behind her and an SS man screaming at the mother of the child. She turned her head back, and the SS man approached her now. "Don't look back," he said in German to Dzidzia. "Go forward faster, faster."

Dzidzia understood German. Her mother had been teaching her German for the last two years. However, she thought now that it would be better not to understand—she didn't want to go faster. She was very tired. Her father took his hand from hers and put his arm around her." It is better to walk this way," he said.

Dzidzia knew that he wanted to protect her better but she wasn't sure if he would be able to protect her here.

She had never doubted the strength of her father until now—until she had heard the voice of the policeman behind her back.

After a very long walk, the passengers of the train came to a big courtyard. They heard music playing.

Music here? Dzidzia was astonished.

"There is an orchestra of women," somebody whispered beside her. After a while the music stopped.

There were so many people that she was afraid of being lost in the crowd. She took the hand of her father again with one hand and with the other, the one holding the suitcase, she took the hand of her mother. It was very difficult to hold the suitcase and her mother's hand at the same time but she wanted to remain with both her parents. Dzidzia didn't pay too much attention to the others around her until she heard people screaming and crying. She didn't know how it happened that she was no longer holding her father's hand and he was now in another part of the courtyard. Had she fallen asleep for a moment? He was standing among a lot of other men. He waved to her and her mother. Dzidzia wanted to run to him but she was stopped by her mother. Dzidzia started to cry.

Lunia tried to calm her.

"Don't cry, don't cry, Dzidzia. You have to be brave."

"I don't want to be brave. I only want to go to my father. When can I go to him?" Dzidzia asked.

"I don't know," answered Lunia. There was sadness in her voice. She gave Dzidzia a handkerchief.

Dzidzia wiped her tears. She noticed the handkerchief was the one her mother saved for special occasions. Was it a special occasion now?

Her mother was caressing her hair as she had used to do at home, and this made Dzidzia think about her home in Tarnow. She knew that there, in Tarnow, she had been a child, but here in Auschwitz, in one hour, she had changed. If somebody had asked her how she had changed, she would not have been able to answer. She only knew that something terrible had happened around her and within her and that she would never be as she had been before.

Dzidzia thought now about her aunt Mundi and her cousin Anita. Her aunt and her cousin lived in Zakopane. They had gotten Christian papers and pretended that they were Christians. Dzidzia had lived with her aunt and her cousin for a few months. It was difficult to be away from her mother and father but she had been told it was safer. Dzidzia longed for her parents, but she sometimes enjoyed living in Zakopane. Zakopane was in the Tatra mountains, and Dzidzia loved the mountains and the forests. She also was happy that she did not have to wear the Star of David on her coat. It was much easier to live without that star. Dzidzia expected to stay longer with her aunt and cousin, but one day a woman told her aunt that she should not take care of a Jewish child. It was true that her aunt Mundi and her cousin Anita looked less Jewish than Dzidzia, but Dzidzia never thought that she could be recognized as Jewish.

"She is not Jewish," said her aunt to the woman, but after that her aunt seemed to be afraid to walk with Dzidzia on the street. Dzidzia began to spend almost all her days inside the little apartment and she became unhappy. Her aunt felt sorry for her but said that she must not take chances, that it was too dangerous for Dzidzia to go among people. Finally her aunt said she thought that it would be better for Dzidzia to go back to her parents in Tarnow, and she was sent home.

Her mother kissed Dzidzia and the kiss reminded Dzidzia of the last night she had spent in Tarnow. Lunia had come to her room and said, "Sleep well, my little one."

"I am no more a little one," Dzidzia said, "but I would not mind if you sang me the lullaby you used to sing to me when I was little."

Her mother smiled. When Dzidzia was very small, Lunia used to sing to her, every night, Brahms' Lullaby. This lullaby became a part of Dzidzia's life. She liked the melody, and especially the words about the sunshine of tomorrow. On the last night in Tarnow, Lunia again sang Brahms' Lullaby to her.

Thinking about the lullaby now made Dzidzia feel very sleepy. Her eyes began to close and, noticing this, Lunia put an arm around her. Thus Lunia and her daughter stood in the courtyard in Auschwitz as night fell, and waited. For what were they waiting? Lunia tried not to guess. She knew that at this moment, for the first time in her life she felt completely abandoned. But what was more important was that her child was abandoned too. With the objectivity of a judge she tried to put together all the facts and reach a verdict for the fate of her child and herself. A few minutes earlier she had still seen her husband in the other part of the courtyard. Now he was gone and Lunia knew that she would never see him again.

Lunia looked at her daughter and thought, she should be sleeping in her own bed. In her imagination she saw Dzidzia's room, brightly decorated with pink wallpaper, the three dolls sitting on the bureau. The room perhaps held more meaning for her, Lunia, than it did for Dzidzia. It was there, before Dzidzia was born, that she had sung lullabies to her son. She had loved her son so very much. And Mulo, as she called her husband, was so proud to have a son. He was a fine baby. Blond with big blue eyes. He looked like all the Goldmans and he was named after Mulo's father, Abraham. He had died when he was nine months old. The baby fell ill and nobody could save him. A few years later, Dzidzia was born. Lunia thought about her son now. She also thought that she had so many plans for her daughter.

Dzidzia played piano and wanted to study music. Now, standing in the courtyard of Auschwitz, Lunia thought about her own music studies in Berlin. She had spent several years there. She had liked the city. She had lived in her sister's house in a very nice district, called Dahlem. Dahlem had many beautiful villas and many trees. Now, Lunia thought about different streets in Berlin. From far away she saw Kurfürstendamm and Unter den Linden. She thought about Berlin's concert halls and Berlin's museums. How could people who were brought up amid such culture build concentration camps? Lunia wondered. She remembered the day when she got her diploma with honors from the Berlin Conservatory.

She caressed Dzidzia's hair and she thought of her fingers. The professor in

Berlin had said that she had hands made for piano. The professor—maybe now he is somewhere in Poland helping to kill Jews. No, Lunia didn't want to think this way about her professor. No, she couldn't believe that every German was a follower of Hitler. Even now, in March 1943, after witnessing the atrocities and having lost many members of her family, she still wanted to believe that not all Germans were the same. However, if they were not all the same, why were they not able to stop the killing of innocent people? Was it possible that all the good people whom she had known in Berlin had lost their ability to respond humanely? For Lunia it was like a nightmare.

Somebody put a hand on Lunia's shoulder. A woman standing near her whispered. "Those of us left here with all our belongings are in danger. A prisoner who passed by a minute ago told me that we will have to go to the showers and we will never come back from these so-called showers."

"What? What showers are you talking about? Why are we in danger?" Lunia asked.

The woman continued evenly: "The guards will ask us first to put our belongings and our clothes in one room and, after, to enter another room with showers. But these showers are not showers. Instead of water they spray poison gas."

Lunia looked at Dzidzia now. If what the woman said was true, she must try to save Dzidzia. Should she wait any longer or try to talk to somebody now? Maybe she could talk to the SS man who stood not too far away. Maybe she should say that her husband was a good doctor and she and Dzidzia would be brought to a safer place. Lunia started to sweat. She became dizzy for a moment. She saw Dzidzia's room, the dolls, her husband, her little son, the streets of Berlin. All mingled in her mind. She trembled. She didn't know what was happening to her.

"You almost fell. Are you ill?" The woman beside her asked.

"No," said Lunia. "I don't know what happened, I felt like fainting a minute ago, but I'm better now."

Dzidzia looked at her mother. "Is everthing all right, Mummy?"

"Everything is fine, my darling." Dzidzia closed her eyes.

Lunia observed her daughter now. She bent down and kissed her cheeks, her forehead, her hair. Dzidzia was very beautiful. She had delicate features, a small nose, beautifully shaped lips and deep dark eyes. Why did my sister Mundi think that Dzidzia looked too Jewish? At this moment she regretted that Dzidzia was with her, that she hadn't remained in Zakopane. However, it was too late to undo the past.

A woman who had spoken German to one of the prisoners was passing by. Lunia decided to speak to her. She would ask the woman to bring to the attention of the guards that her husband was a doctor. She was sure the Germans needed doctors. She shook Dzidzia awake and told her to wait for her. Then she stepped out of ranks and approached the German woman.

"I would be very grateful to you if you could help me. Tell me, please, where I can get information about my husband. He is a doctor and he was taken away from this courtyard just a short while ago. I would like to know where he is and let him know that my daughter and I are still here."

The woman looked at her, complimented Lunia on her excellent German and asked where she had learned it.

"In Berlin."

The woman smiled and said: "I cannot give you any information about your husband and I cannot help you find him. I am sure that you will meet him again one day."

In the eyes of the woman and in the expression of her face there was something evil. Lunia decided not to ask her anything more.

She returned to the place where she had left Dzidzia. Dzidzia asked if Lunia had found out anything.

"Do you think that we will see father again?" she asked.

"I am sure, we will," answered Lunia.

A few hours later after depositing their belongings and their clothing in one room, Lunia and Dzidzia, completely naked, entered the room with the showers. Lunia tried to hold the hand of Dzidzia so they would not be separated. There were many, many women and children, all naked, in the same room.

Dzidzia cried. "I don't want to stay naked here," she screamed to her mother. She had to scream because it was so noisy around. Suddenly the noise diminished. Dzidzia held her mother's hand and softly said, "I am sleepy again. Mummy, please sing me the lullaby."

And Lunia started to sing Brahms' Lullaby. She remembered the words in Polish: *Jutro znow w ranny brzask zbudzi cie slonca blask, jutro znow w ranny brzask zbudzi cie slonca blask.* (Tomorrow again at the morning dawn the shining sun will wake you up.)

*To my aunt,*
*Regina Frisch-Herzig*
*the wife of Dr. David Herzig*
*and the mother of Lonus.*

# Bridge Game

Regina liked Debica. Debica was a small town in Western Poland, and there Regina had spent all her married life. Because she liked Debica she stayed there after her husband, David, a lawyer, died in 1933, and after her son, Lonus, emigrated to Palestine in 1937. She really didn't have any other place to go to. Her parents had died long ago, and her only brother who was taken during the First World War to Russia as a prisoner, had remained in his captors' land. She had never heard from him. Still at times, she missed her brother. She had liked him very much and believed in his talent. He had been a very good violinist, and when he started his concert tour, just before the war in 1913, he was acclaimed as one of the best violinists in Galicia.

Regina remembered how proud her father had been.

"What can be more beautiful than music?" her father had said. "Music is the most profound means of communication and most important, the language of music is universal."

There was something in her family's genes that drew its members to music, more so than to business, law, medicine or science. Lonus played the piano. Regina did not play an instrument but she enjoyed music and she thought that she understood it in various forms. Her husband had also been a music lover. Regina remembered the time just before his death, when they had both gone to Berlin to seek the advice of a famous professor, a specialist in cancer. David had insisted on going to the opera. He was already very ill; he suffered a lot. The cancer had spread to his liver—there was no cure.

"I am sorry, I cannot do anything more," the professor said. "Sometimes nature plays different tricks on people—you may still have a few years to live." The professor knew that what he was saying was not true, but he didn't want to take away hope from David. That very same night, after receiving this cruel verdict, David wanted to go to the Berlin Opera. They saw *The Twilight of the Gods*.

The performance was majestic; the libretto and the music seemed to be one, powerful, grand. David was enchanted, but afterwards in the hotel, he told Regina, "I am afraid of German nationalism. This nationalism is rising and rising, and as much as I admire Wagner, sometimes I feel that Wagnerian opera glorifies the power, the pure German spirit. For me music should unite people and not divide them." Regina never forgot these words.

She was cleaning her small apartment as she thought about David and the night in Berlin. That was in 1932. David died in 1933.

Regina went to the kitchen. In her oven was a small cake she had made with some flour she had received as a gift from one of her friends for babysitting, two eggs and saccharin. We will enjoy our evening, Regina thought.

She had invited for this Purim night her three best friends, a couple and a man who had lost his wife a few months ago. The couple, a medical doctor and his wife, had been helping Regina since the time that David had died. They had adopted her as a member of their family, and she was grateful to them. They were neighbors and she saw them almost every day. The widower, Joseph, was an elderly gentleman, who, at the beginning of the war, had lost his daughter, his son-in-law, and their two children. He really never recovered from his tragedy, but as long as he had had his wife, he thought he had a purpose in life. With his wife dead he was sinking deeper and deeper into depression. Regina knew that in the old days Joseph liked to play bridge, and she decided to have a bridge game for Purim night. They would be four, she would serve ersatz coffee with her cake and for a little while they would escape reality.

The cake was ready. She took it from the oven and the delicate aroma spread through the room. The kitchen seemed gayer than before. One little cake, Regina thought, and the kitchen becomes a kitchen. Many years ago David had said that their kitchen always smelled of good, fine food. It was long ago. David called their kitchen Regina's kitchen, but it was really Zosia's kitchen. Zosia had been their faithful housekeeper. She had been very attached to the family and had helped Regina to bring up Lonus.

Regina's thoughts turned to her son in Palestine. She could endure everything because she knew that Lonus lived in the free world. Even if something happens to me, she thought, it does not matter. The most important thing is that my son will survive the war and will enjoy the world after. She could imagine this world after the war. She knew that the whole of education will be different. After this terrible war people will look for solutions to their differences. Thus, in the midst of all Nazi victories, a widow in the small Polish town of Debica, was drawing plans in her mind for a better tomorrow. She knew that she was not the only one. Everybody had to hold onto something, some spark of hope, because if everybody had nothing but the surrounding reality, everybody would become insane.

Regina left the kitchen and went to her room. There in the mirror, she saw her face. She was fifty-three years old but she looked much older. Her skin was white, her brown eyes had circles under them and her hair was all grey. She observed herself in the mirror with surprise. She didn't pay much attention ordinarily to her appearance but what she saw now upset her. What happened to me? How could I change so much? I really look like an old woman and I am not so old. But, Regina admitted, I am lonely, and loneliness has done this to my looks.

Somebody knocked on the door. Liza, a little girl of eight, came in. "Can I stay here?" she asked. "My mother went to get some bread and she didn't want me to go with her. She said that I would be safer in your place. My mother said that there are new Gestapo men in the city and we can have some surprises."

Regina looked at the little girl. The words about Gestapo men and surprises sounded strange in the childish voice, though the expression and the tone were quite mature.

"Come, come," said Regina.

The child saw the fresh cake in the kitchen.

"Oh, Mrs. Herzig, you have a cake today." She looked at the cake and she moistened her lips with her tongue.

"Yes, I have a cake and I will give you a small piece, but not right away, because this cake is still hot, and I don't want you to have a bellyache."

"Nobody has a bellyache from a cake, but if you want, I will wait, I have time."

"In the meantime," said Regina, "help me to cover the table. I'm having a bridge game tonight. I have to set the table, prepare cards and paper."

"How do you play this game?" asked the child.

"I will try to explain to you. You know what the bridge is. The bridge over the water helps people to cross from one place to another. It brings people together from two shores and allows them to meet. The bridge as a card game is a game between two teams of two players."

"I understand. It is like other games. The team is important. My mother said yesterday that she and I make a good team, because when she is sad, I try to smile, and when I am sad, she tries to make me happy. Is it the same thing in the bridge game?"

"Yes," answered Regina.

"When I am big," said the child, "I want to always have a good partner because I want to win. I hope I will always win, my mother told me that I am a born winner."

Liza again observed the cake. Regina caught her eyes and said: "Now you can have a piece of cake. It is almost ready to eat."

The child sat down on the chair near the table. Regina put a piece of cake on a little plate and handed it and a small fork to Liza. She then gave the little girl a small white napkin. Liza took the napkin and put it near her plate.

"You have so many nice things," she said. "Even this napkin is very pretty." She started to eat. She ate slowly, as though she would prolong the pleasure as much as possible.

"It is delicious," she said. "I like your cake very much."

Regina smiled at the child. She was happy to see Liza enjoying the cake. It really didn't matter that her guests would have smaller portions. When Liza had swallowed her last bite, Regina brought her another piece—a tiny one. She knew that the child would like to eat more. However, Liza didn't touch the second piece of cake. Regina knew that Liza wanted to say something but was too shy to say it.

"What is it, Liza? Don't you like my cake anymore?"

"I love it but I would like to put this piece in a paper and take it to my mother. Maybe one day when we have flour, you can give my mother the recipe for this cake and she can make it." Regina was astonished. She knew that Liza was a good child, but she didn't expect this measure of sacrifice in one so young. Seeing her surprise, Liza said,

"It's like a bridge game, my mother is my partner and I want to be a good partner to her."

Liza laughed and her laughter was like a bird's song in the desert. Regina cut another piece of cake and wrapped the two pieces in white paper.

After a time, when the table was covered with a white tablecloth decorated with colorful cross stitches, when the cards, the paper and the pencils were laid out for guests, Regina sat with Liza in the kitchen.

"Do you know," said Regina, "that today is Purim. At Purim time in Palestine the Jewish children wear all sorts of costumes and sing and dance in the streets? There is a parade of grown-ups and children and this parade is called *Adlojada*. A long, long time ago the Jews were in danger in Persia. They lived in fear, like we live here now, and a day came that a bad man who wanted to kill all the Jews lost his power. Then Jews could live freely again."

"What does it mean, the bad man lost his power?" asked the child.

Regina thought for a while before answering Liza. "It means that the good people didn't want to have a bad one among them and punished him."

"It must be that they had a good team."

Now Regina laughed. "You are right. Queen Esther and Mordechai were a good team and they won."

The child looked at the table with the cards in the room nearby and said: "Everything is like a bridge game—the partners and the teams. Did you have good partners in your life?"

"Very good ones. The best was my husband."

There was a knock at the door. Liza's mother came in.

"Thank you, Mrs. Herzig, for keeping my daugher here," said Liza's mother.

"Don't mention it," said Regina. "I always enjoy having Liza."

"Do you know," said Liza, "that today is Purim and children in Palestine wear different costumes and sing and dance on the streets? Here," the child handed her mother the two pieces of cake in the paper. "This is my treat for you—from Mrs. Herzig and me—for Purim."

"Do you know," said Regina, "that people give gifts for Purim? I have to look for something to give you as a gift, Liza."

Regina went into the bathroom. There, in the medicine cabinet, she found a very small bottle of eau de cologne. "Here," she said. "My gift."

"I love the bottle," said the child. "It is really nice." Regina opened the bottle and Liza smelled the eau de cologne. "Thank you, thank you," she said. "This is the first time that somebody gave me cologne."

"You will think you are a grown-up girl."

"Mummy says that I am already a grown-up, right?" Liza turned to her mother.

"It is true," said Liza's mother. "You are very good and almost a grown-up girl—almost."

Liza kissed Regina and left.

At seven o'clock the guests arrived. They lived nearby and didn't even have to cross the street. They all sat around the table.

Joseph looked at Regina and said, "Do you remember, many years ago, we were together at a ball and we danced a tango called *Skrwawione serce* (A bleeding heart)? There was one line about the bleeding heart being trod on in the crowd. We both agreed that the melody of the song was nice but the lyrics were worthless. However, today, before coming here, I really thought that my heart was bleeding, that I was hurt, that nobody needs my heart and that it is stepped on in a crowd which does not recognize my feelings. We are afraid of feelings now because we have to think of our survival. Do you remember, Mrs. Herzig?"

"*Skrwawione serce*—I remember," answered Regina. She also remembered the words she had said to Liza about her partner in life. Her David had been a fantastic partner. She understood old Joseph, because her heart sometimes also felt trampled on by people who didn't need it.

After a while, the four friends started to play bridge. Each guest had eaten a piece of cake and assured Regina that she was the best baker in Debica. The couple played together, Regina played with Joseph. They all tried to be cheerful and even cracked some jokes.

Around nine o'clock somebody pounded on the door. Regina opened it. Four Gestapo men came in. They asked if Regina Herzig lived there. She answered that she was Regina Herzig.

One of the Gestapo men said: "Look at them, they play cards. The Jews play cards like in the olden times—and they eat cake. Look at them—they eat good cake!" The man threw the remainder of the cake on the floor, then asked the couple and Joseph for their papers. They handed him their papers and waited. The Gestapo man returned the papers to the doctor, his wife and Joseph and ordered them to leave.

"We wanted only Mrs. Herzig," he said, "because she is in contact with England."

"In contact with England!" Regina laughed. She really laughed. It was too absurd. "What are you saying?"

"Yes," said the Gestapo man. "We have reliable information. Your son was in the Jewish Brigade attached to the British Army. He has been captured. He is now in a prisoner-of-war camp in Germany. And you—you have been in contact with the British Government. You will be punished for it—"

Regina didn't hear anything more. She fell to the floor and lost consciousness.

*To my cousin,*
*Lonus Herzig,*
*son of Dr. David Herzig*
*and Regina Herzig.*

# The Shimmy

L onus stopped reading. He could not understand why he was so nervous today. He knew himself quite well and he was not often upset. He had a way of approaching everything at a slow pace. So many times he had heard his mother say, ''Why are you so phlegmatic? Why do you take so much time to make decisions? In life you have to act fast.''

Lonus really didn't know why he was like that. As a youngster he had been called "the Englishman" because Englishmen were supposed to take more time doing things than other people. However, there were certain activities in Lonus' life that proved his ability to move fast if he wanted to. These activities were playing piano and dancing.

Lonus loved music. Music was for him a fountain with a million sources. Since childhood he had been fascinated by the potentialities of music and spent many long hours at the piano. There, touching the white and black keys, he basked in the cascades of tones vibrating in the air like laughter or lost himself in the enchantment of a fairyland of sounds. Sometimes he was able to evoke, with the touch of his fingers, a celebration of life, sometimes the depths of sorrow. For Lonus music was also a way of traveling to far-off lands and places. When he played the Second Rhapsody of Liszt he felt himself being led through Hungarian forests and stopping in delightful Hungarian villages, while glorifying the zest of life. When he played Mozart, he admired a world of sweetness, charm and elegance, of beautiful salons and cosmopolitan people, of cities whose very names bespoke glamour, Vienna, Salzburg, Paris.

But when he wanted to enter a special world, a world of poetry and the sound of rain pounding at the windows, he played Chopin. There was something in Chopin that reminded Lonus of his dreams. He could visualize fields of flowers, old forests, and people trying to grasp the breeze, the wind. Sometimes a sound like thunder would erupt in Chopin's music to remind Lonus of the power of nature. There seemed to be in Chopin the polarities of acceptance and struggle, and Lonus performing on the piano saw in these a guide to facing his reality.

At the moment, Lonus was sitting on his bed. He did not pay attention to the few other people talking in the room. He was in a German prisoner-of-war camp. Lonus had joined the Jewish Brigade in Palestine and was apparently one of the first Jews captured by the Germans. He had been in this camp for more than a year.

He was thinking of his mother in Poland wondering if she was still alive. He was her only son. She had wanted him to be a lawyer like his father and his father's two brothers. In the year that Lonus' father died, Lonus finished high school. He passed his baccalaureate exam with very good marks and entered the law university in Krakow. But he failed in his first year. Often he thought it was because at this time in his life he discovered dancing. Lonus smiled to himself. As Mozart had conducted him through the salons of Europe, as Liszt had taken him through dark woods and quaint villages, so American music, with which he became acquainted during his university year in Krakow, introduced him to the rhythm of the shimmy. There, in Krakow, as an eighteen-year-old boy, Lonus heard jazz for the first time. Once he started to dance the shimmy, he became obsessed by it. Soon he was the best shimmy dancer on the university campus. Still, he was sorry that he had failed his law exams. He had previously been a good student but the shimmy interested him more than Roman law. Jazz became Lonus' life. When he danced the shimmy and shook his body from the shoulders down, he was transported to New Orleans and felt the Negro and Indian and French cultures mingling and giving birth to new exciting rhythms.

After failing the exams, Lonus decided to quit law. He was too ambitious to repeat the year. His mother didn't want to accept the fact that Lonus was mainly interested in music; she didn't believe he should regard music as a profession. After many discussions, Lonus agreed to become a pharmacist. "I will try," he told his mother. In September 1935 he went to Prague. He liked Czechoslovakia but he immediately hated pharmacy. He could not conceive of spending his life mixing different powders and fluids and playing with tiny little bottles. He was sorry for his mother, but he wrote to her that he did not even intend to take his exams and went back to his home town of Debica. He became very popular among the young people. He played all the American blues on the piano, he danced the shimmy and later other American dances. His mother could not understand his betrayal of Mozart and Chopin. However, Lonus told her, "I did not betray Mozart or Liszt or Chopin or even Beethoven; I have only parted with them for a while."

One day Lonus met a group of young men and women who were preparing themselves for pioneering work on the land in Palestine. They were ardent Zionists who wanted to flee anti-Semitism and build their own country. Their ideas appealed to Lonus. He joined the group, took training on a farm near Debica, and in 1937 emigrated to Palestine. First he worked on a kibbutz. The work was hard, conditions were primitive and many of his companions contracted malaria and suffered greatly. After working in the fields, Lonus often traveled in the evening to Tel Aviv to visit with friends of his parents from

Debica. In Tel Aviv he also played piano from time to time. The work on the kibbutz was hard but he enjoyed doing constructive things. He understood also, as an only son, he had been too much sheltered by his parents, and he saw the kibbutz the best apprenticeship for life. He worked long hours, his face became brown now from the sun and the wind, his hands grew stronger. Once when he visited some friends near Kineret they expressed astonishment at his changed appearance.

"You are a strong man," said one of the girls who had known him when he had studied law in Krakow.

"You are not the same, Lonus."

Later in the afternoon he and the girl walked near Lake Kineret. All around it was peaceful and quiet. Silently Lonus admired the waves of the Kineret. He started to think about God. He had never thought about God very much. His parents believed in God, but they were not practicing their religion except at Rosh Hashana and Yom Kippur. They were more interested in Zionism and the rebuilding of the Jewish homeland than in Judaism. It had never occurred to Lonus that he could feel a link with God, but there beside the blue and green waves of the Kineret it happened.

In the evening, when he went back to his kibbutz, he looked at the mirror. He saw dark brown eyes behind his heavy glasses, he saw his small nose, his well shaped lips, and he smiled. The girl was right; he had changed, he had become a man. He also knew that, for the first time since he had come to Palestine, he felt a sense of pride that he worked on the soil which was given to the Jews by God. He was surprised; for the second time that day, he was thinking about God.

Later on, near the window of his room, Lonus heard music. Somebody was playing a *hora* on the accordion. Although he still liked American dances better than the *hora*, he joined the circle of young people dancing outside. One of the girls was particularly attractive. Lonus liked her a lot. Her name was Frieda. She used to tease Lonus that he did not know what to do with girls. She danced with Lonus for a while, and later she went to Lonus' room. She stayed there the whole night. They made love. Lonus knew what to do with women after all; Frieda said that he was a good lover.

After that first night, Lonus and Frieda discussed their lives. Frieda thought that Lonus' place was not in the kibbutz, but in the city. She encouraged him to try to establish himself as a musician in Tel Aviv.

"After all," she said, "music is your first love and the soil, your second."

For a while Lonus really didn't know what to do. He stayed on in the kibbutz but he made a few trips to Tel Aviv to see if he could play there in one of the cafes, to start with. One evening he returned to the kibbutz earlier than he was expected and found Frieda with his best friend. Frieda told Lonus that she was going to marry the friend.

It was difficult afterwards for Lonus to remain in the kibbutz. He took a job as a pianist in a small cafe in Tel Aviv. Every evening he played there, fox trots and the tangoes, recalling as he did so the gay time of the shimmy. But he was not very happy. He lived in a small room. He worked hard. He had to play six to seven hours every evening, and he didn't consider his work pleasant or important. It was impossible for him to go back to the kibbutz. There have been too many failures in my life, he thought, and he continued playing the long evenings in the cafe.

In the meantime, the news coming from the fronts and from the countries occupied by Germans was very sad. When the Jewish Brigade started to recruit young men, Lonus joined it. He wanted to be useful, he wanted to help destroy Nazism.

But he hadn't had a chance to do much fighting before he was captured. It hadn't been his fault. He had been riding in a truck convoy when suddenly his company was surrounded by Germans. And now here he was.

Lonus was so preoccupied with his thoughts that he didn't notice the few people who had entered the hut. They all seemed to be excited.

"What happened?"

Joseph, another prisoner from the Jewish Brigade who was captured with Lonus, said that he had just seen two British reconnaissance planes.

"Our planes," he exclaimed. "Imagine this is the first time that British planes have scouted this place. I am sure they are preparing something. I would like to see them drop some bombs and show the Germans what our side can do. It's marvelous. I see freedom coming."

Lonus smiled now. "Naturally," he said, "we all know that the end of the war is near."

"Come," said Joseph. "Don't stay here. Bombs are bombs."

"Are you crazy?" Lonus exclaimed. "The English planes will not bomb the prisoner's camp. They will certainly bomb the military installations situated not too far from us."

"Listen," said Joseph, "the pilots can make mistakes."

After a while Joseph and the others left and Lonus was alone again. He heard some detonations not too far away. He went outside. The day was sunny, a beautiful March day. He loved the sun but many times during the war the sun bothered him. He knew that it was not the fault of the sun that so many people were killed during the war, but sometimes he could not understand that, on the sunny days, people fight, people are killed. So many times, he looked at the sky and asked the sun "How can you shine?" He often compared the shining sun to mocking light showing the human misery in full force. Again and again he argued with the sun although he loved sun very, very much. Since that afternoon at the Kineret, he hadn't thought much about God. Now, watching the sky over Germany, he thought about God. Why, he wondered, hadn't it occurred to him to ask God why so many people had died and why so many people would die before the end of the war? In the bright sun of this March day in 1944, Lonus tried to answer his questions. The war, he thought, is a matter of man and not of God.

God in man is man's conscience and when people are deaf to their consciences, God cannot do anything—it is too late. God gives to every man his own conscience, and at the moment that this conscience is given, it is up to man to make use of it. If people would listen to their consciences they would not fight—they would try to make room for everyone, because there is a place for everyone in the world. No—Lonus didn't want to argue with God. And he also thought—he has to believe that God exists—yes, he has to believe because of the mystery of the unknown, because of the shepherds playing on their flutes and because of the quiet waves of Kineret.

After a while Lonus went back to the hut. He had always been a dreamer and he wanted to think about the end of the war and freedom. Where would he go? What would he do? First he would try to find his mother in Poland. If she was still alive, he would take her with him to Palestine.

Lonus thought that the only place where his mother would be comfortable in Palestine was Jerusalem, because she didn't like hot summers. The image of his mother grew so vivid in his mind that Lonus felt that he could touch her hand. And later he would travel. He would go to America. He would walk the streets of New Orleans amid the sound of music. He had discussed it once with Joseph. Joseph told him that he would like to see America because he was interested in America's dynamics, those dynamics which allowed the homeless people to build a home.

Lonus was not interested in skyscrapers, he wanted to hear Louis Armstrong and Benny Goodman. He wanted to listen, to listen and dance, to snap his fingers to the beat forever.

"Am I crazy?" Lonus thought. "The war is not over and here I am already planning what I'll see and do in America. However, it is true that I started making these plans the time I danced the shimmy in Krakow."

Lonus was still thinking about dancing the shimmy when British bombs accidentally hit the prisoner-of-war camp killing him.

*To Hela Zarski-Schorr,*
*who was the first wife of*
*my late husband, Sigmond Shore*
*(Zygmunt Schorr), and their son*
*Wlodek (Zev).*

# The Swings in the Park

Tarnowski Street was hilly. Hela and Wlodek walked up it very slowly. Wlodek had turned six just a few days before.

"Why are you walking so slow?" the child asked his mother.

"I am tired," Hela said. Hela was, indeed, bone-weary. She hadn't slept for several nights. She had not been able to fall asleep since Sunday. It was on Sunday that the owner of the apartment where she lived had come to see her and advised her to move.

"It is not so easy to find a place now," she had answered. "Please give me at least a month. During that time I will look around." Hela didn't have any idea why she was asked to leave. She had a very pleasant room in the apartment, which belonged to a worker in the chocolate factory and his wife and she lived there with her son. They had both gotten used to the quiet street and the nice neighborhood. Hela felt safe there. Besides her room, there was a kitchen and a bathroom which she shared with Mr. Jan and his wife, Mrs. Zosia. Hela liked the owners of the apartment. They were gentle people in their forties. They had one son, who lived with his grandparents in Przemysl. He didn't want to stay in Lwow. It was this son's room that Hela and Wlodek rented.

Tarnowki Street was now very familiar to Hela. She knew every house, every tree. On her way to Krasinki Street on which she lived, she always admired the sky. Walking up the street was like moving up to the clouds. However, today Hela was not thinking about clouds; she could only think about moving, and she had no idea where she could find a place. It was in March, 1943, that Hela and Wlodek had come to Lwow. They had gotten very good "reliable documents" stating that Hela and her child were Roman Catholic. The child had fair skin, brown eyes, and brown hair.

"Thank G-d that you have happy eyes," Hela had once told Wlodek. The child hadn't understood why it was so important to have happy eyes.

However, Mrs. Griffel, an older woman in the ghetto, explained to him, saying, "Many Jews have sad eyes and often those eyes betray them."

Wlodek turned to his mother and asked what the word "betray" meant.

"To betray," mother explained, "is like revealing a secret to an enemy."

"And what does 'reveal' mean?" asked the child.

"To 'reveal' means to show something or to talk about something that you are supposed to keep to yourself. You see, Wlodek, we now have to go outside the ghetto. We will take the train and go to a big city called Lwow. There we will keep the secret of being Jewish. Nobody must know that we are Jews. Remember, Wlodek. You must never say to anyone that you are Jewish. It will not be for long. When the war is over, you will be able to say that you are a Jew."

"Will I see my father again?"

"Yes, you will."

At this point Mrs. Griffel interrupted Hela and said to Wlodek. "You see, many Jewish children have sad eyes and cannot change them; your eyes are happy and they will help you in keeping your secret that you are Jewish."

"I am not happy now," Wlodek said.

Late at night, Wlodek could not sleep. He thought about Mrs. Griffel and his eyes. He knew that the next morning Mr. Boleslaw was supposed to come and take his mother and him to the railway station.

It was some days later, in Lwow, that Wlodek was told about another secret he could not reveal. That secret concerned his father. Whenever somebody asked about his father he had to say that his father was taken to the army at the beginning of the war and never came back. This was really difficult. He asked his mother why he had to lie about his father, and his mother answered that it was not a lie but a secret.

"I don't see the difference," the child said.

"But I see," mother answered.

She wanted to explain the difference to Wlodek, but at the moment somebody came into the room and they couldn't talk about lies or secrets anymore.

The most difficult thing was the new names. He had to remember all the time that his mother's first name was no longer Hela but Maria and that his own new name was Leszek. Wlodek liked the sound of Wlodek much better than the sound of Leszek, but it was not up to him to make the choice. Mother said that it was too dangerous to keep his old name because on their new papers they were called Leszek and Maria instead of Wlodek and Hela.

They were almost on the top of the hill of Tarnowski Street when Wlodek saw a young man. He waved to him.

"Who is he?" asked Hela.

"I know him," Wlodek said, "I met him in the park near the swings. He's very nice."

"When was it you met him?"

"Last Sunday. You were sitting on the bench reading the newspaper. I was at the swings, and that's where I met him. He came with his little sister, Antosia. He helped me to swing up, up, very high."

"How is it that I didn't see him?"

"I don't know."

"Did you speak to him?" Hela asked.

"Yes," answered Wlodek. "He asked me what my name is and I told him my name is Leszek. He asked me where I came from and I said from Kolomyja."

"My God," exclaimed Hela, "why did you say that?"

"I didn't know that was wrong. You never told me it was another secret. I also told him that we lived on Krasinki Street."

"Did he ask you anything else?"

"Yes. He asked me if we have a nice apartment and if we are rich. I told him that we have a nice room but that I didn't know if we are rich."

Hela stopped. She was suddenly afraid although Wlodek hadn't really said anything that could give them away. At this moment the young man came up to them.

"Hello, Leszek," he said.

"Hello," Wlodek answered.

"How are you?" But the young man didn't wait for an answer before he turned to Hela. "Pleased to meet you. You have a nice son. And if you want to keep your nice son, you'd better give me all the money you have in your purse. You Jews have plenty of money. Quick, quick, young lady, do as you are told."

Hela tried to compose herself. She looked straight in the young man's eyes. She knew that she didn't look Jewish at all. Of medium height, slim, she had reddish-brown hair which had been bleached ash blonde and green eyes. In all the time they had been in Lwow no one even suspected that she was Jewish. She decided to try to bluff the man out.

"I am not Jewish," she said. "My child is not Jewish, and I don't know what you want from me. If you disturb me any longer, I am going to call the policeman. There is always a policeman at the corner."

The young man started to laugh. "Look at her—a brave Jewish woman and a good actress. Where did you study your role? Was your professor maybe one of those rich Jews who live in a nice home?" He obviously was trying to frighten Hela; the expression on his face was half cruel and half humorous.

The worst of his kind, Hela thought. Wlodek started to cry.

"Why are you crying?" she asked.

"I didn't say anything," Wlodek said. "I only told him I like the swings in the park. I only told him that. What does he want from us?"

"I want money," said the man, "just money, and your mother has plenty of money. Tell her that if she is a good mother and she wants to keep you safe, she'd better do as I say."

In spite of Wlodek's crying, Hela's tone remained firm as she replied: "What do you mean, do as I say? Who are you, in the first place, to give me orders?"

"Who am I?" The young man started to laugh.

"Let me introduce myself. My name is Mateusz Rajda. I am thirty years old. I search for people with money and I earn my living by giving orders to Jews, exactly as I did now. Only I must admit, the Jews I met before you were more cooperative."

"Listen," his voice became clipped. "I am not joking. I mean real business. You give me every zloty you have in that fashionable purse, or this little boy is going with me."

Without losing a moment, the young man took Wlodek in his arms and held him tight.

"Let him go," said Hela. "Let him go immediately."

"Do you still want to look for the policeman? Because I don't have much more time. If you don't give me money this minute, the child is mine. If I take him away with me it's going to cost you not only the money you have in your purse, but everything you have to get him back." The man spoke these last words very slowly.

Hela knew that she had no more time. Wlodek seemed very small in the arms of the man. Wlodek wasn't crying now. He looked at Hela but without any expression. His eyes, however, were covered with a shadow.

"All right," said Hela. "It does not really matter if we are Jews or not. And we're not. But because you threaten me to take my son away, I will give you some money. But, first put him down."

The young man put Wlodek down. Hela opened her purse and handed him two hundred zlotys.

He took the money, put it in his pocket, and slowly said, "This was the first meeting, Madame. I know that we will meet again very soon. I love to be well paid."

When the young man left, Hela and Wlodek remained standing for a long while on the empty street. It was Wlodek who broke the silence. "Mummy," said Wlodek, "are you angry that I like swings in the park, that I spoke to the man?"

The voice of the child was forlorn. He was trying to apologize—he really didn't know for what but he somehow felt that the incident was his fault. If he had not talked to this man—if he had not liked to swing high, high like the little girl, Antosia—they would not be caught. The word "caught," he had heard it so many times. Before they left the ghetto of Kolomyja, his father repeated to Hela, "I hope you will not be caught." Wlodek knew that they were caught, and he was afraid.

"I am not angry at you, my dear son," Hela said. She brushed his hair with her hand.

"What will we do now?" Wlodek asked.

"We will go home and I will give you a good supper."

Hela and Wlodek felt better when they entered their room. The room was full of sun, although it was late in the afternoon. After resting for a while, they went to the kitchen. Mrs. Zosia was cooking soup.

"Would you mind," Hela asked, "if I prepare supper now? Wlodek is hungry and he is quite tired—he wants to go to bed earlier today."

Wlodek didn't say anything. He stood near his mother. It was true that he was tired, but he didn't want to go to bed early. He watched hs mother as she peeled potatoes, washed them and put them into the pot.

"We will have eggs and potatoes today," she said, and she smiled for the first time since the young man had left them on the street. Wlodek was happy to be home.

Mrs. Zosia asked Hela if she could give Wlodek some of her soup.

"Yes, thank you, Mrs. Zosia."

Wlodek sat down at the table and Mrs. Zosia put a small bowl of soup before him. "The soup is very good," he said. "Thank you."

While Wlodek ate, Mrs. Zosia and Hela talked. They talked about the war, about the Arbeitdienst, about the many young Poles taken to Germany.

"They need workers," Mrs. Zosia said. "All their German men, at least the majority, are in the army, and they take our young men to work on the farms or in the factories."

Hela was wondering if she should tell Mrs. Zosia about the young man. Hela was sure that he would soon be looking for her to get more money. However, she decided to broach this subject with Mrs. Zosia and Mr. Jan only after Wlodek was asleep. She continued talking to Mrs. Zosia as before. She asked if she had gotten any letters from her son and Mrs. Zosia replied that she had and that she planned to visit him in Przemysl next Sunday.

After putting Wlodek to bed and making sure he was asleep, Hela went into the kitchen. Mr. Jan and Mrs. Zosia were sitting there.

"How are you Mrs. Maria?" asked Mr. Jan.

"Not too well," answered Hela. "I have to talk to both of you. I have known you for several months, and I trust you. Until today I haven't talked about my past, but I believe the time has come for me to tell you a few secrets."

When she said secrets, she thought about Wlodek. Secrets, secrets—we have too many secrets, Mummy.

Hela told Mr. Jan and Mrs. Zosia that she was putting her life and the life of her son in their hands because she was in danger and there was absolutely no one in Lwow she could trust.

Her story was simple. She was Jewish. She had come to Lwow from the ghetto of Kolomyja. Her husband, an engineer and economist, a textile manufacturer, was in the forest and lived among the partisans. He was a specialist in mining bridges. Hela deliberately talked about her husband because she knew that Mr. Jan and Mrs. Zosia were ardent Polish patriots and admired people who worked in the underground. She thought that by awakening their patriotic feelings she might overcome their fear of having a Jewish woman and child in their home. She related the incident that had occurred that afternoon and described the young man in detail.

When she had finished her story, Mr. Jan got up from his chair. He approached Hela and said: "Mrs. Maria, this man was already here today. He came before noon when you were at the park. He told my wife that we have Jews in our house. He said that he would denounce us. We didn't suspect that you were Jewish, but now that we know, we feel very sorry for you. We will try to help you. When we told you a few day ago that you have to move, it was because we need your room for one of our Jewish friends. You asked us why we wanted you to move and not knowing you yourself was Jewish, we could not give you an answer. Since we know that you are Jewish, we will try to find a suitable place for you. There are still good people in Lwow. I am ashamed that Poles like this young man, who extorted money from you, exist. But I cannot do anything about that. Now go to your room and try to get some sleep. But first prepare the most important things for you and Leszek in case you have to move fast. Just what will fit into a small suitcase. The rest we will bring to your new home. Don't worry, we will find you one."

Hela returned to her room. She took from her closet a few dresses, some underwear, and two pairs of shoes. She also packed a few pairs of pants, a few shirts, and a warm coat for Wlodek. When the little suitcase was full, Hela sat down at the small table. She asked herself what she would now like to do most. Yes, she knew. She wanted to write a love letter to her husband, Zygmunt. She thought about what she would write. She would write about the hours when she waited for him, about when they first met, about their engagement and marriage. Her whole life was Zygmunt, the hours were only meaningful when they were together. She would write to him about their beautiful home, a villa in Pabjanice near Lodz, and about herself being so proud to belong to the finest man in the whole universe. This was the way she thought about him. She would write about the morning when Wlodek was born, the most beautiful morning in her whole life. She would also tell him about the young man this afternoon. She knew that this was not so important, but the memory of her meeting the man was haunting all her thoughts. There would be so much to tell Zygmunt. They hadn't seen each other since last March, and now it was September. She thought about Zygmunt being in the forest in winter. It would be very cold there. However, she was confident that Zygmunt would survive because he was strong. And he had tremendous willpower. When Zygmunt wanted something, he acted according to a plan and he usually succeeded. But he never hurt anybody. He was strong but kind.

With Wlodek sleeping in the room that had become so familiar to her during the past few months, Hela thought of Zygmunt's kindness. It was because of that kindness that she was in this room. One of Zygmunt's friends, a Polish notary, recommended her to Mr. Jan and Mrs. Zosia. As long as the magic hand of Zygmunt takes care of me and Wlodek, we will survive. But that thought could not erase her tears. Zygmunt's friend had left Lwow and she didn't know how to contact him. Then should she write a letter? Hela asked herself. Yes, she would.

She took a piece of writing paper and she started: *My dearest Zygmunt—I would like to tell you that Wlodek grew a lot and he resembles you more and more. He is tall and strong. He asks me often about you and I have told him at least a dozen times how I met you. He says he likes the story. By the way do you know that when I saw you the first time, I thought that even if you would not become my husband I would always remember you as the nicest man I ever met? You entered the room in Lodz and you jokingly said, "who is that little redhead in the corner?" and you smiled. Your smile stayed with me all the time, and stays with me still as I write this letter. I think that I should go to sleep now. I need my strength. I will finish my letter tomorrow.*

Early in the morning, when Hela went to the kitchen, Mrs. Zosia said that it would perhaps be better if Hela stayed at home until Mr. Jan returned from work. In the evening he would try to contact a few friends and find her a new home. Hela thanked Mrs. Zosia and went back to her room. Wlodek got up; he washed himself like a grown-up man. He always wanted to show his mother that he was very clean—like his father.

"Am I not clean?" joked Wlodek.

"Yes, you are," Hela answered.

"I want to be like my father—in everything."

"You will be—I hope so," said Hela.

After breakfast, Wlodek wanted to go to the park, but Hela told him it would be better to stay home.

"But the day is so sunny. Take me for just an hour."

"Better no," Hela said.

Wlodek got out his crayons and started to draw some trees. Between trees he drew two swings.

He was showing his drawing to Hela when suddenly there were noises in the kitchen. Hela heard somebody shouting in German. Then Mrs. Zosia answering in Polish. Then somebody else spoke in Polish. Hela recognized the voice. It belonged to the young man who had asked her for money the day before. He was shouting now.

"You'd better not try to save these Jews, you Jewish aunt. Are you not ashamed to be Polish and to love Jews?"

And then the door opened. Two Gestapo men came in. Behind them was the young man. He smiled. "Come on, come on," said one of the Gestapo men. "You are going with us—*schnell, schnell!*"

"Can I take something with me?" asked Hela. "At least a sweater for my child?"

"A Jewish mother," the other Gestapo man said. "They are all the same."

"But I am not Jewish," said Hela.

"We will see, we will see. Now we are going together to the Gestapo headquarters and there we will have a nice conversation."

Hela noticed that Mrs. Zosia was weeping as they walked out of the apartment.

# Selihot

Michal stood at a desk and prayed. He was holding a prayer book so that the light of the portable lamp would fall directly on the page he was reading. Although his head was slightly bowed, he held himself straight. There are certain people whose character is revealed in the way they move, walk or talk; Michal's was revealed in his posture. He was a person who would never bend—never.

He was a man in his fifties, of medium height, slim, with blue eyes and greying hair. He wore a dark grey suit, a white shirt and a plain navy blue tie.

It was late at night. Silence reigned in the room in which Michal, his wife, Rela, and the young boy, David, lived. David was the son of neighbors who had been killed four weeks before. Michal and Rela had decided to take David in and provide him with a home in the one room they shared. Though they did not have an extra bed, they had a couch and David slept on it.

The fall of 1942 was dangerous for Jews in Eastern Poland. "Actions" took place almost every day. Many people were killed, many disappeared and nobody knew where they were taken. David's parents were shot on the street. Michal didn't know too much about them. They had moved into the house where Michal and Rela lived only a few months before. They had originally resided in Krakow, but at the beginning of the war, in 1939, they came to Lwow, and from Lwow, upon the arrival of the Germans, they moved to Kolomyja. Michal remembered them as being quiet people. On the staircase, Michal and Rela had talked to David's parents occasionally. "David is a good boy," they used to say.

It was true. David was a good boy. He was twelve and a half years old, but he looked younger. "He stopped growing," his mother had once said. "Maybe it is because we don't have enough food for him."

Michal and Rela tried to feed David well. They gave him everything they could obtain. David was appreciative and polite but he didn't talk much. Good morning, good evening, and thank you were all he might say in a day.

Praying, Michal saw David observing him from the couch on which he normally slept at this hour.

"Why are you not going to sleep?" Rela asked him. "You must be tired by now."

"No, I am not tired," answered David. "I cannot sleep." Those are the most words he has spoken at one time since he came here, Rela thought. She was sitting at a table in a corner of the room and resumed reading the German newspaper. For her, German was like a mother tongue. She loved to read, but she hated the paper with its nasty propaganda. On the first page was a picture of Goebbels. She had covered Goebbels' picture with a sheet of paper. She could hardly bear to read the articles, but she could not look at Goebbels. She despised the master of German propaganda.

Michal's eyes rose from his prayer book and took in the photographs placed on the desk. There he saw the smiling face of his son, Zygmunt, together with Zygmunt's wife, Hela, and their son, Wlodek. Beside Zygmunt's photograph was the photograph of his daughter Klara with her husband Lonek and their little daughter, Ritka. The largest photograph was that of his youngest daughter, Marysia. She is a beautiful girl, Michal thought. They are all beautiful, my children.

His eyes wandered from one face to another. His son Zygmunt was his pride and joy. Zygmunt was everything that a father could dream of in a son, thought Michal. He was a fine man, a real *Mench*, noble, kind and strong. These days he was a partisan in the forest. Michal thought that strength and kindness were the most important of his family features. It was true that it had not been easy for him to instill these qualities in his children because the mother of Zygmunt and Klara, Maria, had died when Zygmunt was ten years old and Klara eight.

Zygmunt was born in 1909, Klara in 1911. During the First World War Michal was in the army and his wife and children lived in Vienna. Maria first became ill in Vienna. She had heart failure. Michal didn't know of this until he returned home and then just after the end of the war he tried to do the best he could for her. He went with her to Switzerland to consult the best doctors in Europe. She stayed for many months in a sanatorium in Vevey.

"I cannot live here alone, I have to see Zygmunt," Maria told him one day and Michal fulfilled her wish. A week later Zygmunt was sent to Vevey and enrolled in a private boarding school there. When Maria died soon afterward, Michal didn't know what to do. After a year, he decided to propose to the younger sister of Maria, Rela. She was a fine girl. She was already engaged and supposed to marry a young man, but when she heard that Michal wanted to marry her, she broke off the engagement. She felt it was her calling to replace Maria as mother to Zygmunt and Klara.

Klara became very attached to Rela, but Zygmunt refused to accept her in her new role. For him existed only one mother, the mother who had wanted him in Vevey. He was eleven years old at the time, a warmhearted boy and he never offended Rela, but kept his distance from her—all the time. Then Marysia was born. She was the only child that Michal had with Rela.

And now Michal turned to David and said,

"I think that you should go to sleep, you will be tired tomorrow." He looked at the boy and a wave of warmth passed through his whole body. He remembered Zygmunt when Zygmunt was twelve. One day he asked his son to show him how strong he was.

"Do you really want to know?" Zygmunt asked.

"Yes."

Then Zygmunt came to the table and, with his fist, hit the wooden table in the dining room. The table broke. After this incident, Michal asked Zygmunt never to show people how strong he was. The father was afraid of an evil eye. Zygmunt laughed. Now Zygmunt is in the forest, he became a partisan, thought Michal.

Michal walked over to David. He put his hand on his head and asked him to come to the desk. The boy followed him. He stood at the desk, pale, with his very sad eyes, and he seemed to be frightened.

"Why are you frightened?" asked Michal.

The boy didn't answer.

"Why are you frightened?" Michal said again.

This time David looked straight in Michal's eyes and said, "Because I am alone."

Michal knew he had to say something, and without delay, "You are not alone," he said.

"Oh, I know, you and your wife are very good to me—but I am alone."

He stated this with a sudden strength, a strength that seemed to spring from despair. Michal brought him a chair and asked the boy to sit down. Michal sat down also. They were sitting now, one near the other, their arms almost touching.

Michal looked at the boy and said, "Listen. I will try to convince you that you are not alone."

"How? How can you?"

"No one is ever alone. God is with us. God is with you and me, and Mrs. Schorr, and my son in the forest."

"Where is God?" asked the boy. "I am twelve and a half years old and every day, no matter how difficult it was, my father taught me a portion of the *Haftorah* for my Bar Mitzvah. We carried the books with us because my father said that the Germans would not change his mind and he wanted his son to have a Bar Mitzvah. Where is God? I am alone. My parents are dead—I will never have a Bar Mitzvah. My father wanted so much that I know how to pray."

"Do you know how to pray?" Michal asked.

"Yes, I know."

"Then you know, David, what we will do now—we will pray together. Today is a night of Selihot."

"I know how to pray," said the boy, "but I don't know what Selihot is. I only know that there is a prayer called Selihot which Jews say a few days before Rosh Hashanah.''

"Then," said Michal, "you at least know something. Selihot is also a name of the period of days before Rosh Hashanah when that prayer is said. It means 'supplications.' I will try to explain more to you.''

"Where did you learn?" asked David.

"In the Yeshiva, in the Rabbinical Seminary, in many places. You see I was supposed to be a rabbi, I come from a rabbinical family, but after finishing my studies, I decided to go into business and I never became a rabbi.

"Listen," said Michal, "Selihot are the prayers for forgiveness. A man pleads to God for mercy. The prayers of Selihot reflect Jewish suffering, but at the same time show that during the worst persecutions the Jews were always faithful to God, and in their prayers they affirmed their sense of belonging to God. These prayers are the continuation of the psalms. Do you know what the psalms are?''

"Yes," answered David. "Psalms are the songs which people sing for God.''

"Psalms are a beautiful kind of poetry," Michal said. "The Selihot also contain such poetry. Do you know what is poetry?''

"Poetry is a special way of describing the sky or the stars," David said. "It is like seeing a castle in the clouds. My mother liked poetry very much. Once she showed me a flower and said that every man sees a flower differently, but when somebody is a poet, he can describe in a beautiful way the flowers dancing in the wind. But tell me, how could somebody write poetry about people who are suffering?''

"You see, exactly as people can describe the flowers dancing in the wind, people can describe sadness, and tears, and hope like a ray of the sun. Did you ever hear about the great Jewish poet who lived long, long ago in Spain, Yehuda Halevi? Yehuda Halevi resembled David, our king. He wrote about the suffering of the Jewish people, but he also presented the glorious future in his beautiful poems. He believed that after suffering the Jews will experience joy. Yehuda Halevi was born in Toledo. When he was very young, he received a good Hebrew education. Later, as a mature man, he experienced persecution. Alfonso VI, the Christian ruler of Castile, provoked the murder and slaughter of Jews in Castile. Seeing the suffering of his people, Yehuda Halevi decided to give them strength through his poems. During the period of Selihot we say many prayers—hymns composed by Yehuda Halevi and other great poets like Ibn Gabirol and Ibn Ezra.''

The night in Kolomyja was calm. The air was pure and clear; it was a quiet night almost without any motion, without any wind, any rain. In the air of the city where many people lived in anxiety and fear, prayers were heard. Some people uttered them with their lips, and some just with their hearts. And the prayers mingled with dreams about a better tomorrow in spite of the cruel present. In a small room on the second floor, an older man tried to explain God to a boy twelve and a half years old, and suddenly God and the night of Selihot became more powerful than the Nazis and the war. A man and a child talked about Yehuda Halevi. It was Yehuda Halevi who visited the Polish city under the German occupation and brought hope.

"Tell me more about Yehuda Halevi and Selihot," said David.

"Yehuda Halevi wrote many, many poems about suffering and grief, but he loved life. His poetry describes smiles as well as tears, victories as well as defeats."

David interrupted Michal saying, "I know that life is full of tears."

A moment of silence followed David's words, then Michal continued. "When Yehuda Halevi saw how the Jews were suffering, he decided to sing about the Promised Land. He became a singer of Zion. His poems and songs were an expression of love for God and for the Land of Israel."

"Were there many Jews before us who suffered like we do?"

"Yes. Many Jews suffered before us, but as you see, we exist and we never ceased to believe in the God of Abraham, Isaac and Jacob. For many centuries we suffered, but nobody could take our faith in God away from us. We are not alone and the day may come when our suffering will remind people of their responsibility towards one another."

"Does that mean that we still have to praise God, even in suffering?"

"Yes," Michal answered. "You see, Yehuda Halevi described in his songs defeats changing into triumph. And because Yehuda Halevi loved freedom, he sang about Zion and Jerusalem. In the last years of his life Yehuda Halevi decided to go to the Holy Land. There is a legend that Yehuda Halevi, while he was singing one of his most beautiful poems, 'Ode to Zion," was stabbed to death by an Arab before the gates of Jerusalem. But though Yehuda Halevi was killed centuries ago, his voice still resounds with the voices of many Jews singing his hymns of Selihot. And if we are able, you and I, to sit here and pray, if we can forget the world around us, it means that we are strong. We know that this war will end; we can go on and on, as long as we have among ourselves Yehuda Halevis and Ibn Gabirols and others who lived before us, who live among us, and who will come after us and will glorify the name of God."

"Can we pray together?" asked the boy.

Michal took a little navy skullcap from the desk's drawer, placed it on David's head and got up. David got up also, and together they started to pray: *Aschrei yoschvey beytecha, od yehalelluha sela. Aschrey haam schekaha lo. Aschrey haam sheHashem elokav. Happy are those who dwell in Thy house; they are ever praising Thee. Happy the people who are so situated; happy the people whose God is the Lord.*

Some weeks passed. More people were killed or disappeared. A day before

Sukkoth, Michal, Rela, and David were taken by SS men to the train station. When they got there, there were already many people in the train.

The train was so crowded, it was difficult to breathe. Michal didn't feel well. His heart was bothering him; he also felt his blood pressure was high.

"You are all red," said Rela.

"It must be because it is so hot here," Michal said. However, he knew that it was his blood pressure. He didn't want to think. He wanted a cigarette more than anything else in the world. When he thought about that fact, he realized that even the strongest man remains always a man with weaknesses and vices. It was very difficult to approach the window. However, Michal did. A Polish railway worker was passing by. Michal saw him, called to him. "Do you have a cigarette?"

"Yes, I do," said the railway worker.

"Could you spare one?"

"Sure." As the worker was handing the cigarette to Michal, Michal took his gold watch from his wrist and gave it to him.

"Take it," said Michal.

"Thanks," said the worker, and he took the watch from Michal's hand.

Rela looked at Michal but did not say a word. Michal tried to smile but he could not. Somebody gave him a match. He smoked half of the cigarette and saved the other half for later. He put it in his pocket. The train started to move. Michal stood by the window. They were passing by forests. He thought about the land that he had owned nearby, and about a villa in the mountains. There, in Tatarow, his family and he had spent many pleasant summers. Michal loved the countryside. While looking at the passing fields, Michal regretted that he had not spent more time in the country. He didn't want to think about his present because he knew that his present was running out. This bothered him less than he would have thought. He was only sorry for Rela and David. David had become very dear to him in these last few weeks.

After a few hours, the train stopped. All the passengers were told to step down. There, in a small village, they proceeded towards a big barn located not too far from the station. A truckload of SS men accompanied the procession of Jews. On the narrow country road, the people moved slowly. There were women and men, old and young, children and babes in arms. They marched one after another in silence. On the Polish fields in autumn you can see many birds— crows, sparrows, ravens. Michal tried to focus his attention on the sparrows. They were so delicate and small. All these people here on their way to death would be happy to become sparrows, he thought, little sparrows who are often hungry but fly free.

After a short while, the procession came to a big barn. They were ordered into it. It was full of hay. The barn did not have any windows, only an opening in the roof.

When everybody was inside, the SS men shut the door. People started to cry.

"They will burn us here," somebody said, "they will burn us here!"

Michal held his wife's hand in his hand. He put the other hand in his pocket. There, waiting for him was the saved half of the cigarette. As he touched it he wondered, will I ever smoke this cigarette to the end?

Somebody tapped him on the shoulder. It was David. He leaned toward Michal and whispered in his ear, "Thank you for that night of Selihot."

In memory of Klara Schorr-Kanfer,
the sister of my late husband
Sigmond Shore (Zygmunt Schorr)
and Ritka, the daughter of Klara
and Dr. Lonek Kanfer

# The White Gloves

K lara held the white gloves in her hand and smiled. She didn't know how the white leather gloves had found their way into the small two-room apartment where she now lived with her husband Lonek, and her daughter Ritka. She had found the gloves while looking for her stockings in the dresser drawer.

I certainly don't remember taking them with me on the journey here, she thought.

Ritka, Klara's little daughter, was playing in a corner of the room. She was trying to dress her doll in one of her own dresses which she had outgrown.

"Mummy," called the child, "please help me. I need a belt for my dolly, this dress is much too big."

"Yes," Klara said, "this dress is too small for you but too big for your doll. But don't worry, I will fix it in a minute. Let me get a needle and thread and I will try to be a good dressmaker."

"You are not a dressmaker," said the little girl. "How could you try to be one?"

"You see, Ritka, if it is difficult to find a dressmaker, you have to try to be one yourself. If it is difficult to find a shoemaker, it's the same thing. Do you remember, the other day, how I fixed your shoes because I couldn't find a shoemaker anywhere nearby?"

"Maybe you are right," said Ritka. "If you don't have a dressmaker, you have to try to sew yourself. But you know, Mummy, if you don't have a doctor and you need help, you can't be your own doctor. Nobody can be a doctor like my father."

The voice of the little girl was filled with pride and wonder. She looked at Klara as if challenging her mother to disagree with her.

"You are right," Klara said. "Nobody can take the place of a doctor especially a good doctor like your father. But sometimes people do try to be doctors if there aren't any doctors around."

Ritka shook her head and repeated, "Nobody can be a doctor like Papa."

At that moment she saw the white gloves in the hands of her mother.

"Let me see those gloves, Mummy. Aren't they beautiful? Where did you buy them? I never saw them on your hands." The child took the gloves from her mother and touched the soft, shining leather. "Mummy, these gloves—are they silk?"

"No, they are a very fine leather. When you touch them you think you are touching silk."

"Where did you get them?"

"Your father bought them far away from here and a long time ago, before you were born, Ritka."

"Where did he buy them?"

"In Paris."

"Where is Paris?"

"Paris is in France."

"Can you tell me about Paris?"

"Yes, Paris is a beautiful city. It's the capital of France."

"Is it like Warsaw before the war?"

"Yes," said Klara. "Like Warsaw. But it's also a very special city. Every street is different. There are big, wide avenues like the Champs Elysées, there is one of the most beautiful squares in the world, La Place de la Concorde, and there are narrow, old streets where you can see artists sitting and painting. And people walk along the banks of the River Seine, which flows through the middle of Paris."

"Will you take me one day to Paris?" Ritka asked.

"Certainly."

"And what will you show me there? What will you show me first?"

"First I will show you the Eiffel Tower, a very high tower from which you can see all of Paris."

"And after?"

After that we will go to the Jardin de Tuileries and play with many children of your age."

"When can we go?"

"I don't know," said Klara. "After the war."

"And when will that be?"

"I really don't know when the war will end," Klara said.

Somebody knocked on the door, and Klara opened it. Olga, her neighbor, came in. Olga was young and lived alone. Her husband had been taken away by SS men a few months before, and since that time she hadn't had any news from him. In spite of that, she hadn't lost hope and kept saying "Shimon will come back, you will see."

Not only was Olga's morale high, she was busy all the time. She helped in the dispensary, the center for sick Jews. Sometimes she cooked the meager meals for sick people and delivered them, even to distant streets, and sometimes she took care of small children in the vicinity when their mothers had to go on important errands. Klara admired her, her resiliency and strength.

She greeted Klara and Ritka and said: " I just saw Dr. Kanfer. He told me that he will not be back until late because he has to spend time with a patient who had a heart attack."

"Who is it?" asked Klara.

"An old lady, Mrs. Rubinstein," Olga said.

"I know her," said Klara. "She is the mother of one of my husband's best friends, my husband is very fond of her."

"That's what I thought," said Olga.

"I never like when Lonek comes home late—it is so dangerous to walk late at night, even with his special permit."

"Don't worry," said Olga. "Dr. Kanfer is appreciated even by the worst of the Gestapo in this city. He is a fine doctor and they know it."

"Yes," said Klara, "but how often does it happen that before you have a chance to show your permit, you are shot on the street."

Olga didn't say anything. She stood at the door.

"I hope that you can stay with us a while. Did you have your supper, Olga?" Klara asked.

"Yes, I did."

"We just finished ours and Ritka was supposed to go to bed, but she insisted on waiting for her father. It is her father who tells her bedtime stories every evening. Now," Klara turned to Ritka, "you have to go to bed. I will wash you, you will brush your teeth, and you will go to bed like a big girl."

"Okay," said the child. "But will you tell me a story? You didn't finish telling me about Paris and the white gloves."

Olga then saw the white gloves on the chair. "My God," she said, "these gloves remind me of another world, of big ballrooms, of opera houses, of a time long gone. Gone but not forgotten."

Klara observed Olga. In her face was anger mixed with strength—but there was not a trace of bitterness—only anger, strength, and determination.

Almost as though she were reading Klara's mind, Olga said, "I believe that I will survive because I love life beyond any imagination, and also I want to survive because of my love for those who were killed, and for my husband who disappeared. If life will spare me, I want to remind the world that no one—no one can wipe us out completely. And I want also to remind the world that I will never hate anyone. I can't hate."

Klara looked at Olga. The expression on her face had changed. There was a radiant sweetness in her eyes. Her lips were half open in a smile. Olga approached Ritka, kissed the child and caressed her hair for a while. Klara observed a shyness in the movements of Olga's hands—the shyness of people who want to show emotion toward children but are afraid of children's reactions.

Ritka's reaction was spontaneous. She took Olga's hand and said, "Can you stay with us and listen to my bedtime story about Paris and the white gloves? Mummy will tell us the story and we will listen."

After being washed and brushing her teeth, Ritka lay in bed under a pink quilt. The room was chilly, and the child had covered herself so that only her little head, resting on a small pillow, showed.

"In the other home, where we lived before, I had my own room," she said. "I never slept in the same room with my parents, but here it is different. I love to sleep in the same room with my mummy and my papa."

"Bedtime story time," said Klara, and then she began:

"It was not so long ago. My husband and I were on our honeymoon in Paris."

"I know what a honeymoon is," said Ritka.

"Honeymoon is the time after the wedding."

"You are right," said Klara, "but if you interrupt me any more it will be too late for the story."

"All right," said the child. "I will not interrupt you any more. I will be quiet."

"It was not long ago," Klara repeated. "One day your father and I decided to go to the opera. It was to be a gala evening—everybody would be splendidly dressed. Your father, Ritka, said that he wanted to see me dressed as beautifully as I could be. He asked me to wear my long gown in black lace. I had the black satin pumps to go with it. I was happy that I had everything necessary for the evening. In the afternoon, however, when I came back from the hairdresser, I looked for a pair of gloves which I thought I had brought with me from Poland and I could not find them. It was already four o'clock in the afternoon. Your father, Ritka, smiled and said, "I am going to buy you a beautiful pair of gloves, you will see. I hope you will approve of my taste. From the window of our room in the beautiful hotel, I could see your father walking on the Rue de la Paix, one of the most fashionable streets of Paris. Half an hour later he came back and he had these long, white leather gloves. Ritka, you thought these gloves were made of silk. I also thought that they were silk gloves and this made your father laugh.

"Even when I buy you leather gloves," he said, "I want them to be as soft as silk."

Klara spoke these last words almost to herself. For a moment it was as if Ritka and Olga were not in the room.

Then Ritka said, "Did you enjoy your evening?"

"Very much," answered Klara. "We went to the opera—we saw *La Traviata*."

"Will you tell me about the opera?"

"Not tonight, because it is very, very late."

"Please tell me just a little bit."

"All right," Klara said. "The actress who played the role of Violetta was beautiful and her singing was the best."

"Violetta," repeated the child. "That is a pretty name. When I have a daughter, I will call her Violetta." Ritka closed her eyes and quickly fell asleep.

Klara and Olga left the room. They turned off the light and walked to the dining room.

"Would you like something to drink?" Klara asked. "I have some chicory —it tastes like coffee. Try it."

"No, thank you," said Olga. "I'd better go. I have to get up early tomorrow. I have to take care of two children whose mother is sick. Good bye, Klara."

"Good bye, Olga."

Klara locked the door after Olga left. She felt tired. She would like so much to take a bath, but the apartment didn't have a bathroom. She washed herself as well as she could in a big basin, and climbed into bed. She fell asleep almost immediately.

And Klara dreamed. She was somewhere on a street in Paris and everybody around her wore white, silky gloves. She could not see the faces of the people, only their gloves, gloves, gloves. She was running and crying, "Help me! Help me!" Then someone said, "I am wearing white gloves. I cannot help you, because I don't want to make the gloves dirty." Klara cried more and more. And she heard other voices saying: "We are wearing our white gloves—we have to be careful, careful." Then Klara found herself in London. On Trafalgar Square she approached a man and told him she needed help. "Help me," she pleaded. "I am afraid for my husband, for my child—help me!" This man also wore white gloves. He smiled, showed her the white gloves on his hands—and again she saw crowds of people wearing white gloves. In a panic she ran and ran until she came to New York.

She was walking down Fifth Avenue and the people there were also wearing white gloves and singing: "The world wears white gloves and doesn't want to be disturbed by suffering. The world wears white gloves." Suddenly someone screamed, "We can't bear the red stains, the red stains." "What red stains," asked Klara. She heard somebody laughing, "The red stains are the stains of blood," said a voice. "The red stains are blood," a choir of voices repeated. "Go away, go away, don't disturb us. The world wears white gloves, the world wears white gloves."

Klara was standing in the middle of Times Square in New York. She looked around and saw only white gloves. They seemed to have a life of their own. They crowded around her and all noise stopped. Silence reigned, the terrible silence of white gloves. Klara thought that this silence was worse than any screaming she had ever heard.

"Listen, listen to me!" she begged. "Please, we count on you, people of the world. We count on you."

But there were no people, only white gloves. The whole world was deaf. Nobody had heard her voice. She was sick of the gloves.

"Why are you wearing these white gloves?" Klara asked the man who stood beside her. The man didn't answer. Then Klara repeated her question: "Why are you wearing these white gloves? Please tell me, Sir."

"I am wearing these gloves," said the man, "because I want to spare my hands."

"No," said Klara. "I know why you are wearing them because they act like anesthetics, they make you numb and you don't feel anything. If you did not wear these gloves and your hand touched mine, you might understand what suffering means. The warmth of my hand might awaken your human feelings, you might try to help. Please take off your white gloves, please."

The man smiled. He had a terrible, cynical smile. He spread his hands so that Klara could see every finger in the white leather.

He said, "But I don't want to touch your hands, your hands don't exist for me."

Klara ran at the man. She wanted to scratch his face, but the man grabbed her hands. And as he did so, Klara felt his hands through the white gloves. They were cold—like ice. The man smiled. "You see?" he said. "The whole world is silent and cold. I am like the rest."

Klara wanted to go back to Poland, she didn't know which road to take, she was tired of pleading to the conscience of the world. She wanted to go back to her husband and her child. Now she screamed: "Let me go back! Let me go back!"

When she woke up, Lonek her husband was holding her in his arms. He kissed her face.

"What happened?" he asked.

"I had a terrible dream," said Klara.

*In memory of
Dr. Leon (Lonek) Kanfer,
the husband of Klara Schorr-
Kanfer and father of
Ritka Kanfer.*

# The Promise

P lease promise me, Papa, that you will come for lunch today. Please promise.''

The little girl stood up on her bed. Thus standing she could reach her father's face. Holding his face now in her little hands, she repeated, ''Please promise me, please promise me.''

Lonek smiled. He was tall, strong and handsome as his daughter had often told him. He had never before heard a child compliment her father the way Ritka did.

Often he laughed and turning his face to his wife, Klara, would say, ''I wish you would see me the way Ritka does.''

One day Klara answered: ''Oh, maybe I see you the same way, but I keep it a secret to myself.''

Lonek smiled at his daughter and said: ''A promise is a promise; I will be here at 12.30 for lunch. And I hope that my little girl will be without fever the whole day. Tomorrow you will be allowed to leave your bed.''

''Great!'' exclaimed the child, ''and after tomorrow we will go for a walk.''

''Maybe,'' said her father.

Ritka lay down again. Lonek covered her with the pink quilt. He kissed her and left the room. He went into the kitchen, where Klara was washing dishes. He touched her wet hands, ''I never saw you work so hard. Day after day, I see you losing weight, and I don't know what to do.''

''Don't worry,'' Klara said, ''Another week, another month, and things will go better for us. And one day—after the war—when you work like you used to work, I will take it easy and gain weight again.'' She was laughing.

''Do you want a plump wife? Really plump?''

''I want a healthy wife. Healthy and happy.''

''How could I not be healthy with such a fine doctor as you beside me, and how could I not be happy, having the most handsome husband in the whole wide world.''

She wiped her hands with a towel and embraced Lonek. Next to him, she seemed very tiny. Lonek was over six feet tall, with brown eyes and prematurely grey hair. He looked like an actor who plays the role of Don Juan all the time. But appearances are deceiving—he was utterly faithful as Klara knew.

Before the war he had been the assistant to a famous professor, a specialist in internal medicine, and he was considered one of the best diagnosticians in spite of his youth. During the war, first under the Russians and then under the Germans, he had worked as a doctor; and until now he had felt protected by their need of him. However, a few days before, the situation had changed. A new commando came to Kolomyja, where Lonek had lived with his family for several months, and deportations were occurring every day. Lonek could see the beginning of the end of the Jewish community in this city.

He kissed his wife, grabbed his small bag of instruments, and rushed down the stairs. He remembered that he was supposed to visit old Mrs. Rubinstein. He looked at his watch. He had promised Ritka he would be back at 12:30 for lunch. It was now 8 o'clock. The house where Mrs. Rubinstein lived was not too far from his place of work. Though he was still permitted to practice a few hours in the hospital, he spent most of his time in a little room provided by the Jewish community where he treated Jewish patients. Lately, Lonek's work had become very difficult because the community lacked many basic medicines.

On the street, Lonek saw a few SS and few Gestapo men. He tried to walk faster. His Star of David armband was on the left sleeve of his coat and he pushed it down and held the bag of instruments in such a way that this sign of Jewishness was partly hidden. It is easier to walk this way, he thought. At least I won't be stopped on every street by the guardians of the Nazi order. But each time he hid his armband, he felt ashamed. It is, he thought, like escaping from myself, and I never wanted that. I was always very proud to be a Jew.

He remembered the many times he had discussed with his brother-in-law, Zygmunt, the need to show the world that Jews are strong and proud. Lonek and Zygmunt belonged to the Revisionist organization which promoted the creation of a Jewish battalion during the First World War and held that Jews had to know how to fight with arms in their hands for freedom and for a homeland in Palestine. Wladimir Zabotinski, the founder of the organization, had been a personal friend of Zygmunt's father and Zygmunt had been strongly influenced by this Jewish leader. Lonek realized that the Revisionist ideal was no more than a dream in present circumstances where Jewish life was at stake every day. Still, he didn't want to give up the dream, even in the worst of times, because he believed that as long as he had it, he would be able to face the cruel reality. He recalled words which Zygmunt had said many years before: "We have only one way to make Palestine our home—we have to learn how to fight and we have to learn how to win."

Lonek remembered that when he heard Zygmunt's statement, he had thought that perhaps the time had come for Jews to leave their holy books for a while and take up rifles. But should Jews leave their holy books especially now, under the German occupation, when they are persecuted for their sense of belonging to their God? And can they? Lonek asked himself.

As on a movie screen, he saw in his mind the small rooms where little Jewish boys were taught since the expulsion of Jews from the Holy Land; he saw the academies in Spain and Germany where Jewish thought flourished; he saw people for whom the words of God became a way of living. How many Jews, thought Lonek, feel God more than three times a day when they pray? He who finished his studies of medicine and who was only partly exposed to Jewish learning, knew that the covenant with God, which started in the Sinai desert, was strengthened every day by this eagerness of the Jews to learn, to be with their God consciously, spiritually.

Again he thought about Zygmunt. Zygmunt went into the forest and fights as a partisan. Zygmunt had kept his promise. One day he had said:

"I will not die without fighting."

How about me? It had never occurred to Lonek to leave his wife and his child as Zygmunt had done. One reason was that Klara looked Jewish, unlike Zygmunt's wife, Hela, and she could not pass as a non-Jew.

Zygmunt's wife had taken a chance. She obtained the forged documents for herself and their little son Wlodek and lived somewhere as Roman Catholics in the free world. Once Hela and Wlodek lived as Christians, Zygmunt felt free to join the partisans in the forest.

Would I leave Klara? Lonek asked himself. Never, he answered his question. We have to try to survive together. And then an idea flashed across his mind. Whatever happens, he swore with a terrible certainty, he will not die without fighting.

He was coming now to the house of Mrs. Rubinstein. There was a crowd of people around the front door.

Lonek tried to push through.

"Don't go in there," somebody warned him. "The Gestapo is inside." The people in the crowd were talking loudly. There seemed to be no Jews among them, only Poles and Ukrainians. A woman approached Lonek.

"Wait, Doctor," she said. "Why do you want to enter the lion's mouth?"

"But I have a patient in this house, an elderly woman. She had a heart attack just a few days ago. Mrs. Rubinstein."

"I know her," said the woman, "but if I were you, I would not go in unless you are looking for trouble."

At this moment a young boy appeared on the street. He was maybe sixteen or seventeen years old. Lonek knew him. He was Marek, the son of friends. Marek saw Lonek, stopped beside him and whispered, "Don't stay here. I ran away from our house. My parents were taken away this morning."

Lonek didn't have time to ask him anything. Marek entered a house on the opposite side of the street.

The woman who had previously warned Lonek approached him a second time, and said, ''I assure you that Mrs. Rubinstein will not need any medical help any more. Please go away. I have seen too many Jews taken away. I am not Jewish, but I care for people.''

A young man who heard her last words, smiled and taunted her: ''Another traitor—she cares for Jews.''

The woman didn't answer. She took Lonek's hand and slowly they both left the scene.

She is holding me like a child, thought Lonek. Why is she doing it? At that moment two trucks stopped nearby. The trucks were full of SS men.

The woman asked Lonek to enter a small building.

''I live here,'' she said. ''Please stay with me until the street is more quiet. Don't go now.''

Lonek went into the building. He thanked the woman for bringing him to her apartment.

''You are a very special lady. There are not too many people who care— who care for Jews,'' he said.

''But I do,'' said the woman. ''I believe in God.''

After Lonek left the woman's apartment, he didn't know if he should go to the hospital or to the Jewish Center. He decided to go to the Jewish Center. The Jewish Center was nearer. He walked fast. He passed two streets. They were almost empty. On the third street he saw several trucks loaded with people. Each truck was surrounded by SS men. Where are they taking them? Again he tried to decide whether to go directly back home or continue on to the Jewish Center. I am sure they need me at the Center, he thought. He tried to avoid the main street. When he got to the Center, there was nobody there except one mother with a sick child.

The mother cried, ''I came here and I didn't find anyone. What happened to all these people?''

''Show me your child,'' said Lonek. ''What is wrong with him?''

''He has fever,'' said the mother.

Lonek took the boy of four or five in his arms and put him on the table in his little office. The lad was very thin; he had blue eyes, blond hair—he was a beautiful child. Lonek examined him.

''He has flu,'' said Lonek. He opened his bag and took out a few children's aspirins.

''Please give him this aspirin and make him drink a lot of water. Keep him warm.''

He had hardly finished his words when two SS men came in. One said to the woman, ''Follow us.''

Lonek looked at the SS men and said: ''This child is sick.'' The mother started to cry. One of the SS men took the child in his arms and laughed. ''A Jewish bastard with blond hair and blue eyes is sick.'' He put the child down. He laughed again.

"And you?" He asked Lonek. "Who are you?"

"I am a doctor."

"Herr Doktor," the SS man said. "A Jewish doctor treating a Jewish child. We don't need Jewish children but we still need the Jewish doctors."

"Leave her—leave her here," said Lonek.

The second SS man touched the first on his arm.

"Leave them," he said. "We have more important things to do. Anyway, we will find them—if not today, then tomorrow. You know as well as I do that they can no longer escape."

Everything happened so fast—as suddenly as the two SS men had appeared, they left.

Lonek was still standing with the aspirin in his hand. The woman stopped crying. She dressed her child; she took the aspirin and went to the door. Before leaving, she said, "God bless you—you are a fine man, Dr. Kanfer."

When the woman had gone, Lonek looked at his watch. It was already late— 12 noon and he promised to be home at 12:30. He went down the stairs. He looked around. Everywhere he saw the trucks with people. Many times in the past months he had witnessed "actions," but he had never seen so many trucks as now. He started to walk fast. A young SS man stepped out from a big apartment house and walked toward him. Lonek saw the trooper and started to run. He ran as fast as he could. He heard shouts, then one shot, two shots. He didn't turn his head. He kept running. After a short while he stopped at the corner gasping. He looked back—nobody was following him. He resumed walking. He knew that it was dangerous to pass through the streets full of trucks waiting for people, or loaded with people. He knew that it would be better for him to go to some of his Christian friends and hide for a while. But he didn't want to leave Klara and Ritka alone. Besides he remembered that he promised Ritka he would be home at 12:30 for lunch. Even now, facing imminent danger, Lonek thought it was important to keep one's promises.

Finally, he reached his street. A truck full of people, neighbors whom he knew well, was parked at the corner. He heard somebody shouting, "Dr. Kanfer, Dr. Kanfer, don't go home!"

The voice shocked him at first. He realized that he didn't want to believe that his family was in danger. He entered the house in which he lived. He climbed the stairs. He opened his door. Two SS men were emptying every drawer in the dining room. He didn't pay them any attention and they paid no attention to him. They were too preoccupied with their work.

In the bedroom Klara was dressing Ritka. When Lonek entered, Ritka exclaimed, "I knew that Papa would keep his promise."

Lonek took his daughter in his arms and asked Klara, "What is going on? Why are you dressing Ritka?"

Klara was calm. "We have to go," she said. "The two men who are in the next room told me that we will leave the city and we will be taken to a better place."

"Papa," asked Ritka, "are you going with us?"

Klara answered her, "No. Papa is a doctor. Papa will stay here."

"What are you saying, Klara? You really think that I will let you go without me?" He tried to smile but he could not. "Don't you remember that we promised each other always to stay together, no matter what? My life and yours and Ritka's are one—remember!"

Lonek left the room. The two SS men were still plundering Lonek's and Klara's possessions. Even Ritka's toys were on the floor.

"What are you doing?" Lonek asked.

"We are just examining your wealth," said one of the SS men. "We are only interested in articles of value. You really don't need them anymore."

"What are you doing here?" Lonek asked again.

At that moment a third man entered the room. The two SS men stopped emptying the drawers. They both stood straight now. Lonek understood that this new SS man was their superior officer.

"*Schnell, schnell* (fast, fast)," he said. "Don't lose precious time. Take these Jews down. The truck is waiting."

"They are not going down," said Lonek calmly. "My daughter and my wife are staying with me."

"Are you crazy?" said the SS officer. "Who are you?"

"I am a medical doctor. Here is my German identity card."

"Oh—yes. You can stay, but your wife and your daughter will follow me and the others—they are not medical doctors."

"Papa, Papa," Ritka called. Lonek left the room and the three SS men. Ritka was dressed now. She looked lovely in her pleated navy skirt and white sweater.

Lonek took her in his arms and said to Klara, "You are not going. You are not going."

Now Ritka smiled. "Papa always keeps his promise. He said that we will always be together."

Lonek looked at his child and at his wife. The three SS men were still in the next room. Lonek knew that he could not escape. However, he decided he would do anything to save his family. He put Ritka down.

"Stay here," he said to Klara. He returned to the room where the three SS men were evaluating the contents of the drawers.

"Take everything," Lonek said, "but leave me my child and my wife."

"Why?" asked the SS officer. "Why should we leave them here if we have an order to take all the women and children today? Who needs women and children?"

He pushed Lonek aside. He went into the bedroom where Klara and Ritka were waiting. He grabbed Klara's hand and pushed her before him, just as Lonek returned to the room.

The SS officer didn't expect to be attacked. Lonek slapped his face once, twice, then kicked him. He doubled up and fell to the floor. The other two SS men rushed in and grabbed Lonek from behind. He fought with them, he was taller than them and very strong. And as he fought, he heard two shots. The SS officer had fired the shots at Klara and Ritka. Lonek saw his wife and his daughter on the floor. He didn't stop fighting. There were three men now—and suddenly a fourth entered. This SS man had a dog. Lonek didn't want to give up fighting. He had nothing to lose. He had lost everything already. His wife and his child were dead. He was still fighting when he heard the man with the dog say:

"This Jew is not worth a bullet. My dog will take care of him."

*In memory of Maria
(Marysia) Schorr
the sister of my late husband,
Sigmond Shore (Zygmunt Schorr)*

# The Railway Station

Marysia stood by the window. She didn't know how many hours she had been there; she only knew that her husband was supposed to be back two days before, and he hadn't come back.

He could have phoned, Marysia thought, and he didn't. That means something has happened to him. No, I can't believe that. He has to come back. He is the only one in the whole world I have—the only one.

Zdzislaw, Marysia's husband, was a Pole, a Roman Catholic. Marysia loved him. After she lost her parents, Michal and Rela Schorr, after she lost her half-sister, Klara Kanfer, after her half-brother, Zygmunt, went into the forest, after many other relatives were killed or vanished, Zdzislaw was the only person who really kept her alive. Marysia was twenty-two and a half years old but she had lost her interest in life.

"How can you say that you don't care for life," her husband asked. "How can you, knowing that I love you so much?"

Zdzislaw had married Marysia in the worst of times, when Poles were being persecuted for helping Jews. But Zdzislaw didn't care about that. He loved Marysia and had tied his life with hers.

"You will survive," he told her. "If not for yourself, then you will survive for me."

Marysia was beautiful. She was tall and slim. She looked very much like her half-brother Zygmunt except that her eyes were brown rather than blue. She had a very fair complexion, light brown hair, a small, finely shaped nose, and small but sensuous lips of a raspberry color.

"You will never need lipstick," Zdzislaw teased her, "because lipstick would be less bright than the color of your lips."

Marysia knew that she was loved. In fact since her childhood she had been surrounded with love. Her mother was the second wife of her father. The first wife had been her mother's sister and Marysia had been named for her. There was something special in the way her father treated her—he had loved his first wife very much. She knew about that. Her own mother was respected by her father and by the children of his first wife, but she was never really loved by them. Marysia from her early years on, gave her mother special attention, as if to compensate her for this lack.

Marysia's life was pleasant until the war. When she finished high school and passed her baccalaureate examination in May, 1939, she thought that she was the happiest girl in the world. She wanted to study languages. She planned to go to Paris to study French and then to London to study English. Her half-brother Zygmunt encouraged her.

"You should see the world, and before settling down, learn to enjoy life." Often he teased her saying: "I tell you, go to Paris, to London, to New York, because I have confidence in you and know that you will always behave yourself and carry on the family's principles."

Though joking, Zygmunt was right. Marysia had no taste for amorous adventures. Often while talking to her girl friends, she would be surprised at how many of them had secrets, even slept with boys. She was not interested in having their kind of experiences, she just wanted to live a decent, fulfilling life, to learn, to increase her knowledge, and one day to settle down with a fine husband.

When the Russians came, her whole world collapsed. Her parents had to move out of their home. Because her father was the owner of a big store, some houses, a sawmill, and timberland, the family was made to suffer. According to the Communists, Marysia's father was a rich man and rich men had to give the government everything they possessed. The Communists also had regulations forbidding former property owners from living in big cities and Marysia's family had to move to a small town, called Kolomyja.

There during the Russian occupation, Marysia met her future husband. He was a teacher. First they became friends. Zdzislaw lent Marysia various kinds of books; he even taught her French. Though he was only a few years older than Marysia, Zdzislaw was very mature. He had helped his mother, a widow, since his early years and had always been a serious person. When Zdzislaw met Marysia, his life changed.

"It was as if the sun entered my heart," he said.

The parents of Marysia didn't object at first to the friendship but when Marysia revealed to them that Zdzislaw was more to her than a teacher, they became very unhappy.

"He is not Jewish," said her father.

"But he is a good man," Marysia answered.

This was the first time in her life when she knew that she hurt her father, and she was filled with regret. But it was too late to alter the situation. Gradually her father's attitude changed, Marysia was surprised. She had expected that he would fight; he was a very proud Jew.

One day, several months later, he said to her: "You told me that we live in different times now. I have thought about that. I know that you are right. But different times do not give us a permit to throw out our past. However, I will let you make your choice.''

Marysia suffered. She decided to stop seeing Zdzislaw. Zdzislaw, although he, too, was pressed by his mother to break with the Jewish girl, did not give up hope. He tried on several occasions to speak to Marysia's father, but somehow he always failed. He once even went to Marysia's house, but he was politely refused when he asked to speak to the father. Marysia's mother told him that Mr. Schorr was not well.

Several more months passed. The Germans supplanted the Russians. One day Zdzislaw announced to his mother that his whole goal in life was to save Marysia's life and that he intended to marry her and bring her into their apartment to live. Zdzislaw's mother was dumbstruck. She didn't talk to Zdzislaw for a week. But when the week was over, she cried and she said that she wanted her son's happiness.

One day, after a thousand Jews were taken to an undisclosed destination, Zdzislaw went to Marysia's house again and this time he was able to talk to Marysia's father.

''Mr. Schorr,'' he said, ''I love your daughter. Look at what is happening around us. Every day people die. Marysia is young. I will take her with me, and I promise you that I will take care of her. Let me marry Marysia—please, let me marry Marysia.''

Marysia's father asked Zdzislaw to wait a few days; he wanted to think. Those few days became terrible. From every Jewish home, people were taken. One night, Michal Schorr called Marysia to him and asked her if she was ready to marry Zdzislaw. He warned her that the marriage would mean that she would have to become a Catholic.

''I don't know,'' Marysia said. ''I don't want to convert although I love Zdzislaw very much. I know that for a Jewish father the conversion of a child is very painful; it is as if he loses the child. I don't want to lose you, Father, and I don't want you to lose me.''

Afterwards Marysia's father repeated their conversation to Zdzislaw. Zdzislaw said that he understood. He also said that he had a solution. He would get forged documents for Marysia. The priest who would marry them would not know about Marysia's past, and when the war was over, Marysia could then decide if she really wanted to convert or not.

Zdzislaw kept his promise. He obtained the forged documents, and one day he went with Marysia to a small village and married her there. The priest suspected something unusual, but he didn't ask any questions, and even provided the necessary two witnesses, peasants from his parish.

Marysia never went back to see her parents. It was too dangerous. Occasionally, Zdzislaw visited them. Marysia's parents urged Zdzislaw to leave the town. They thought that Marysia should not live in a place where everybody knew that she was Jewish.

However, it was not easy for Zdzislaw to leave Kolomyja where he worked in a notary office since the schools had been closed, and where he had organized secret classes for young people and taught Polish literature and French. Marysia spent all her time at home, waiting for Zdzislaw, reading and teaching herself French and English. Sometimes Marysia helped Zdzislaw's mother prepare the meals. The rest of her time she sat by the window, watching the autumn turn into winter.

And that is how she saw all the Jews in Kolomyja being taken to the railway station. She was sitting by the window and one after another the trucks loaded with people roared by. She wanted to run after them. She didn't care any more for her life. She ran to the door, but Zdzislaw's mother forbade her to leave the apartment. Zdzislaw's mother was stronger than Marysia; and she stood in the doorway and held Marysia with both her hands. Afterwards, Marysia's arms had black bruises.

Zdzislaw tried to apologize for his mother.

"She wanted to protect you—please understand."

No, Marysia didn't want to understand her. She loved Zdzislaw, but when the moment came that all the Jews were taken from the town she wanted to be with her people.

This happened on the day of Hoshana Rabba. Marysia knew that Hoshana meant, "Save us." When she was a child, her father had told her that on the day of Hoshana Rabba, the Books of Judgement, which are sealed on the Day of Atonement, are put away until the next year. Now Marysia repeated:

"Hoshana, hoshana. Save us, save us." In her own words she begged that the Books of Judgement should not be put away but reopened, and that the verdict of death be changed to the verdict of life. Marysia asked God for help, and later she thought that God had heard her plea but that man had not harkened to God. Why did God give so much power to men? Marysia asked.

For Marysia could not blame God. Being the daughter of a proud man and a proud Jew she had been taught that the responsibility for the destiny of the world is in the hands of God and men, and on earth men have to know how to treat one another. "God gave us commandments, his teachings," her father had said, "and the rest is up to us."

It was on Hoshana Rabba that Marysia's parents were taken away and killed. And it was also on that day in autumn that something died in Marysia, and was swept away like the autumn leaves, which fall and are carried to their resting places with the wind.

From that day onward, Zdzislaw's mother never left the front door of their apartment open. The door was kept locked. And when Zdzislaw was away, working or out of town, Marysia stayed locked in the apartment. Marysia knew that Zdzislaw's mother was really her friend, but she felt like a prisoner.

Marysia looked out the window. It was cold outside and snow was falling. She was alone and suddenly she became frightened. Zdzislaw hadn't come back as he had promised. His mother had left early in the morning. Maybe she already knew that something had happened to Zdzislaw and she hadn't told Marysia. Marysia wanted to do something. She must do something. Yes. She wanted to help Zdzislaw if he was in danger. God, she thought, I don't have anybody but Zdzislaw. The whole world seemed to be empty. Somewhere in the sky Marysia saw clouds, many, many clouds. They were small and big, grey and white. Clouds are not lonely, Marysia thought.

She decided to go to the railway station. Zdzislaw had gone to Lwow to find them an apartment. He thought that it would be safer for Marysia there. Nobody knew her in Lwow and she could be free to move about. But Zdzislaw hadn't returned from his search.

Marysia looked for her purse. There were 200 *zlotys* inside. She took out the money and dressed herself. She got a sweater and a heavy coat from her cupboard. It was the first time since the previous winter that she would wear these clothes. The sweater was blue—her favorite color and the favorite color of her father. The coat was grey with a collar of Persian lamb. After putting on the coat, Marysia donned a woolen hat and a shawl her mother had knitted for her. She wrote a note for Zdzislaw's mother then tried the front door. It was locked as usual.

She went back to her room, she opened a window and climbed through it. The apartment was on the ground floor. She jumped. She fell in the snow. Her knee hurt her a little. Now she was standing. She breathed the fresh air and she felt drunk. She knew that it was dangerous for her to stand outside; everybody knew that she was Jewish. For a second she hesitated—maybe it really was better to go back to her warm room and wait for Zdzislaw or his mother. She stood for a while. She touched the snow. The snow melted in her hands. She had forgotten her gloves. No, she would not go back. It was as if a hidden force was pushing her to go to the railway station. In her imagination, she saw trains coming in and rushing out, coming in and rushing out. She knew that Zdzislaw would be on one of these trains and she wanted to wait for him, there at the railway station. The railway station was for her like a magnet now and she started to run. She heard somebody calling, "Look at her, she is Jewish—she is Marysia Schorr!"

She ran for a long time until she reached the station. She sat down on a bench near the rails. Somebody approached her and asked her what she was doing there.

"I am waiting for my husband," she said.

She didn't know how long she sat on the bench. Many trains came in. One arrived from Lwow. She looked at the face of every passenger who got off it. No Zdzislaw.

Night came. Marysia was still sitting on the bench. A railway worker approached her and asked her to come into the waiting room. "It is too cold to sit here. Come. Please," he said. Marysia refused. She wanted to sit there outside and wait for Zdzislaw.

A day later Zdzislaw came back. He had been retained in Lwow on an important underground mission. When he entered the apartment he found only his mother.

"Where is Marysia?" he asked.

"I don't know."

"What do you mean you don't know? I asked you never to leave the door open."

"I locked the door, but our neighbors say Marysia went out through the window. She went to look for you. She left me a note. It says: 'I don't want to be alone in the world. I am going to the railway station. I will wait for Zdzislaw there.'

Zdzislaw rushed out. He ran to the railway station. He asked people if they had seen a beautiful young woman there the day before. Yes. Some workers had seen her but they did not know where she had gone—she had disappeared. One worker said:

"I tried to convince her to go home but she said she was waiting for her husband. That is the only thing I know."

Zdzislaw never found out what happened to Marysia. The railway station kept her secret.

*In memory of Herman (Hesio)
Neuschuller, my beloved friend,
whom I will not forget until the end
of my days. (The excerpts from the
letters are authentic, translated
from the original Polish.)*

# A Bridge Over Hate

Hesio was sitting at the desk. He was alone in the office. It was quiet and peaceful all around. Hesio stopped working for a while. He knew that he was supposed to finish two important drawings before tomorrow. However, he needed the relief of expressing his feelings in a letter to Rena. Hesio loved Rena. He had loved her from the first moment he had seen her, a few years before. Rena represented for Hesio a world of hope, of dreams, of poetry, of song. There was something in Rena that allowed him to cross the frontiers of his own life into a world he could only imagine.

Hesio was an engineer. He was a specialist in building bridges. Hesio's professors appreciated his talents. After obtaining his diploma, he was offered a prestigious position in Zaleszczyki, near the Polish-Rumanian border. There he built a bridge which was considered one of the finest bridges in Poland. While building it, Hesio tried to preserve the beauty of its surroundings and when the bridge was finished, it looked like a part of the landscape, created by nature and not by human hands. Hesio was praised, especially because he was then only twenty-six years old. Hesio was precise and meticulous as an engineer should be but he was also sensitive to beauty and it was this sensitivity that drew him to Rena.

Rena was all sensitivity. She awakened feelings in Hesio which revealed to him an unknown part of his being. Often, listening to Rena's words, he realized that his enchantment with life was enhanced by their being together. Hesio met Rena in the summer of 1938. Rena was sixteen. She had come to Brzezany to visit her uncle, the pharmacist, Emil Goldman. After Hesio was introduced to her, he heard that Rena had been interested in a young doctor since her fourteenth year. He didn't let that discourage him. He promised himself that when the appropriate time came, he would find a way to Rena's feelings. What he didn't foresee was the war.

Hesio didn't see Rena from the summer of 1938 until one December day in 1939. It was during the Russian occupation. Rena came again to Brzezany for a few days. Hesio saw her on the street. She was walking with another girl of her age. As Hesio approached them, he was so astonished to recognize Rena that he didn't even greet the other girl whom he knew well. Rena looked at him, smiled and said that she was glad to see him but that she was leaving Brzezany the next day. Hesio had never before felt so forlorn, especially after he heard that Rena was still interested in the young doctor.

When Hesio met Rena for the third time, the whole world was changed. Rena came with her parents to live in Brzezany in September, 1941, when the Germans were already there. Rena's family, her father, mother, brother and she had had to leave Lwow. They had very little money and thought that it would be easier for them to live in a small city, where rents were cheaper and it was easier to get food. Rena was then nineteen years old, but she hadn't changed. She was cheerful, full of hope and confidence that the night of the war would pass and the dawn of a bright day would appear.

This time Hesio said to Rena that it was destiny that had brought her to Brzezany, that his relationship with her would give his life a new dimension.

"This new dimension must be love," Rena said. "If it were not me, it would be another girl. You talk about dimensions because you are an engineer."

She refused to take Hesio seriously in the beginning. One day Hesio asked her if she was still thinking about the young doctor. Rena looked at him and said, "You know that Marek is far away. He was taken to the Russian army. Let's not talk about that now."

For several weeks Hesio and Rena met every day. Rena's parents liked Hesio and approved of the relationship. For Rena's twentieth birthday Hesio bought her an oven. This gift was received as a blessing, because in the room where Rena and her family lived there was only a small gas burner. After celebrating the occasion with slices of bread with jam, Hesio and Rena went for a walk. Then, for the first time, Hesio told Rena that he wanted her to be his wife.

"I love you," Hesio said.

It was cold outside, November 17, and Hesio and Rena walked together for a long time. In 1941, although many Jews had already been taken from the city, shot or put in prison, it was still possible to walk on the outskirts of Brzezany. Hesio and Rena stopped near a small creek. There, on a very small bridge, Rena said, "You know how to build the most modern bridges. Could you build a huge bridge over hate—a bridge over our enemies, over the mountains of suffering?"

Hesio bent down and covered Rena's face with kisses. Then he looked at Rena's round face and rather plump body, her words about the bridge still singing in his ears and said: "My little Rena, for you I will try to build such a bridge."

Before Christmas time, in 1941, Rena's family was on the list of people who were to be taken away by the SS but they were saved by a miracle. They contacted Polish friends in Jaslo, where they had lived before the war, and these friends sent a car for them on Christmas Eve. A few weeks later a former client of Rena's father (who had been a lawyer before the war) provided the family with Christian papers. From January 1942 on they lived as Christians.

Rena worked as a secretary in the lumber mill; her brother worked there, too. At first they lived apart from their parents, but after a while their father and mother joined them, and the family settled in a small village, Surochow, near Jaroslaw.

"God," Hesio thought. "Today is already May, 1943." He hadn't seen Rena for more than two years, but they were corresponding all the time, and Rena's letters helped Hesio to believe that one day after the end of the war, they would be together—forever. Together, forever. Was he sentimental? Yes. Hesio thought that he was. In spite of all the atrocities, all the inhuman behavior of the victorious Germans, he hadn't changed in that respect.

How happy he was when, a few weeks before, somebody mentioned Rena's songs. She loved to compose songs and sing them at the piano. She was able to convey the caresses of a summer breeze and the mystery of the snowflakes. There was something magic in her. This was Rena. Her name was not Rena anymore— her name now was Lena. "Lena, Lena," he repeated several times. He never used the name Lena in his letters—he was always writing, my love, my beloved, my dearest.

In one of her letters, Rena had asked him to leave the city. She said that she could help him obtain forged documents and work "as Christian." But he didn't accept the offer. He didn't think that he could play the role of somebody that he was not. Was he right? He also remembered that one day Rena's father said, "I don't want to take the Christian papers. What will happen to all the Polish Jews will happen to us." Rena objected—she asked her father to consider taking the forged documents because, as she stated, she did not believe that by remaining as Jews, the family would contribute to the well-being of other Jews. Finally, after facing the immediate danger, Rena's father consented to take the false documents and live as Christians. Now, on May 31, 1943, Hesio thought for the first time that Rena was right. To try to escape death was legitimate. To live as Christians was also dangerous, but at least, the challenge was taken instead of waiting for the verdict of death.

A few weeks ago Hesio was tempted. He wanted to phone Rena and say, "Try to help me," but when he went home and saw his mother and two sisters, he realized that he could never leave them behind.

The Germans had given him an important position as the town engineer, and for the time being even his mother and sisters were protected by his papers.

Hesio looked around. He had a nice office. On the premises where he worked, there were five other people—one other Jew, a draftsman, three Polish employees and the German director.

Lately Hesio had discovered that one of the Poles, the secretary who had come from Lwow, was Jewish. Nobody knew about that. She had, like Rena, Christian papers. She had lost her whole family.

The girl was short with a pleasant face—she didn't look Jewish, and for several weeks Hesio didn't suspect that she was. But one day, when they were alone, she said to him, "I have to tell you something. I have no one to talk to. I want you to know, because you are Jewish, that I am like you.'' She told him how her parents and her brother were killed in Brody and how she was able to save her own life.

Hesio opened a drawer in his desk. He wanted to write to Rena. He usually wrote to Rena two or three times a week and she responded as frequently. Rena's letters were the highlights of his life, and he knew that his letters meant as much to Rena. They were both meeting young people—they probably even had feelings for these people, but Hesio knew that what existed between Rena and him was unique, that no other relationships could tarnish their love. Now, writing, Hesio imagined an afternoon after the war. He wrote that when he would enter their home at five o'clock in the afternoon, Rena would be waiting for him. He described their future home and saw it as a promise of happiness. Yes, Rena and he were ready for happiness. Where would they live? He lifted his eyes from the paper and saw the English dictionary. He had been studying English almost every day. The English language was very important to him. After the war, he thought, he would leave Poland. There are too many graves here, Hesio thought. He wanted to live far away from Poland, far away from Europe. Europe was, is, and always will be fragile. Europe is a continent of eternal conflicts because no nation here wants to respect another. Hesio wanted to take Rena after the war and go to America.

It was not easy to make the decision, because Hesio's brother, a pharmacist, had emigrated to Palestine in 1935, and Hesio was very attached to his brother. However, the United States had attracted Hesio even more since his youth. He thought about building bridges in distant America—so vast—with so many possibilities. In his imagination he saw himself in New York, Washington and San Francisco. He had never been to America, but he admired the dynamics of the country, which was built on a foundation of freedom. Besides, he also thought it would be fascinating to live in a country of speed, of progress. He stopped in his thoughts for a moment. How good it is, he thought, to imagine America in Brzezany—in 1943. The awareness that the free world still exists allows me to dream. . . .

Somebody opened the door. Halinka, the secretary, came in.

"What are you doing here?'' asked Hesio.

"I came back because I forgot a book here. I cannot stay at home without having something to read—I feel so alone. Here in the office, when I work, I really forget who I am—sometimes I really think that my name is Halinka, I forget that my previous name was Blanka. I live in this make-believe world, and as long as I take dictation from my boss or type on the typewriter, everything is fine. But the moment I am in my room, I see myself in the ghetto in Brody, in my hometown. I search my memory for the days gone by, and from each corner of my room the eyes of my dear ones stare at me. They are with me—they don't ask me for anything—they are not jealous that I am alive, but they are there—and they stare and stare at me.''

"Sit down," Hesio said. "I never suspected that you live all the time tormenting yourself. Do you know why your parents and your brother stare at you? They watch you because they want you to survive—they want you to continue. They are proud of you—you are them. Do you understand? You are them. They will not be forgotten as long as you survive. I think that the greatest tragedy of a human being is to die and have nobody, nobody to remember him."

Halinka closed her eyes for a moment. After a while, she looked at Hesio. Hesio got up from his chair. He went to the window.

"If I die," he said," I hope there will be in the summer breeze a word of love which I repeated millions of times to the girl I loved, that in the morning dawn she will feel my wish for the happiness we could not share. If I die I want to be remembered. Everything cannot be forgotten, and maybe my love for Rena will be my posterity. Maybe my love for Rena will teach her that life—no matter how difficult it is, is beautiful."

"Who is Rena?" asked Halinka.

"Rena is the girl whom I love. Maybe it is good that we talked tonight. We live in dangerous times, You, Halinka, have a better chance of surviving than I do. If something happens to me, please take this English dictionary and send it to Rena. I want her to have a remembrance of me. I tried to learn English because I wanted to build a beautiful life for her, somewhere in a more beautiful and peaceful part of the world. Rena knows that I am a good engineer and know how to build. One day she asked me to build her a bridge over hate."

Halinka repeated. "A bridge over hate." Then she took a piece of paper and wrote Rena's address on it. She promised to inform Rena if something happened to Hesio and to send her the English dictionary.

When Halinka left, Hesio resumed writing his letter. Halinka's visit had changed his whole mood. Hopefulness had fled and now he could only think of the danger. He was careful with his words. He tried to avoid saying anything that would touch on the situation of Jews in Brzezany. He was afraid that somebody might read his letter in the office where Rena worked. He only mentioned that the situation was tense. At the end of the letter he wrote:

> Sometimes I think, how long will all this last? I think of you—what you are doing now, at this moment—and how long do we have to be separated. Sometimes it seems to me that at any moment I will take a road to you—that all this which exists now is only a nightmare—that I will go tomorrow, no, not tomorrow, but today. Alas, my open eyes see the terrible greyness of our days. We can only bow our heads and wait. The question is only—for how long? I had a sad day today. The despair is immense. However, I don't want to see the future in black. Our motto is everything will be fine and this has to be so. Be well. I kiss you.

A few days later, Rena received the letter. She read it once, twice, and then she put it away together with Hesio's other letters. They were all together—so many of them—all written between December 24, 1941 and May 31, 1943. One of them fell on the floor. Rena picked it up. It was dated September 14, 1942. Hesio had written:

> My dearest one,
> Only today I received your letter dated 9 of this month. I read this letter several times. I smiled at you, imagining you sitting near the desk, near this white page and writing to me. I was fascinated with every one of your beloved words. I held this letter in my hands and I was envying this soulless object which felt your warm breath, which was enchanted with your deep eyes and was taking your thoughts into itself—when, in the meantime, I have to be satisfied only with a reflection of an image.

Rena left off reading the letter: then she read a few sentences on the second page, a few on the third page. How sorry she was that they had been separated for more than two years. She stopped at one passage and read slowly:

> Now when I have a better moment I dream about finding myself near you and putting my arm around you—and going somewhere and letting ourselves be overwhelmed consciously by one thought only—that we are together. In a letter that was lost and which you mentioned today, you gave me a rendezvous at 8 o'clock one evening. This is such a pleasant and loving idea. I accept. One evening, the 22nd of this month, we will sit near our desks in our offices and we will write our letters. We will see what we will think at the same time and we will find out if our rendezvous is successful.

The letter was long—on each line different words revealed the feelings of a man who cared for her deeply. At the end of the letter, Rena read

> "And now I wish you good night—I kiss you."

A few days later, Halinka informed Lena that Hesio together with his mother and his two sisters, Pola and Frydzia, had been killed. Halinka wrote that Hesio had an important document that could have saved his life but had refused to use it. He had preferred not to leave his mother and his sisters alone.

On many pages of the English dictionary was written: Rena-Lena, Rena-Lena, but Halinka didn't keep her promise. Rena-Lena never received Hesio's English dictionary.

*In memory of my aunt,*
*Runia Herzig-Bross, the sister of*
*my father*

# Knitted With Love

The long shawl was on the floor with all the other things. The room looked as if it had been a field of battle. The drawers of the dresser were pulled out, their contents strewn everywhere. The bed was undone. The pillows thrown on chairs. Runia sat down. She still couldn't believe that the two SS men who had come to the apartment where she lived with her family were gone and had not taken her with them. A few minutes before, she was sure that they would carry her off. However, she was not afraid; she only prayed to God that the members of her family wouldn't return to the apartment before they finished their search. At first, when the two SS men appeared, Runia was frightened. She was sure they would find the two guns she had hidden; and as she observed the men in the search, she prayed God that her husband, her daughter and her son would not come home earlier than usual. She looked at her watch. It was four o'clock in the afternoon. She was so happy to have this watch. It was now the only watch in the family. Her husband's watch had been taken a year before by a policeman, her daughter's watch had been sold one day when the family didn't have any food, and her son's watch, which had been stowed away to be sold in a similar emergency, had been filched just a few minutes before. But thank God that they took the watch and not the guns. If they had found the guns, the whole family would be dead.

Runia got up and started to clean the room. First she folded some of her stockings, her lingerie, and a few sheets and put them in a drawer. Then she tried to get the drawer into the dresser. My God, how impractical I am, she thought. Instead of putting in the empty drawer first, I fill it up and of course it won't fit into this huge old dresser.

Runia paused in her work. She sat down again on a chair. She was breathing fast; she didn't know if this was a delayed shock reaction or just her usual palpitations. My heart does not know how to behave, she thought. It does not listen to me. Nobody listens to me anymore.

Yesterday Tusia, her daughter, had told her:

"Please let me be me. I want to be useful. I want to fight. I will not be killed like thousands of others. If I have to die, at least I will resist and kill before I die.''

Runia could not believe her ears. Her daughter, twenty-one years old, saying that she would kill.

"What?" Runia asked her. "Kill?"

"Yes, I want to kill the killers before they kill me.''

Then Tusia took from the inside pocket of her coat a small revolver. She handed it to her mother and said:

"I count on you—nobody will hide it better than you."

Later she said: "In our city there are more people of my age who have guns. For the time being we're hiding them until the day when they will be used—all at one time.''

Runia didn't ask anything more. She didn't want to know. She knew that whatever she might say would be wrong and the strange thing was that even while trembling for the safety of her daughter, she suddenly approved of what her daughter was doing. Tusia was young, strong and beautiful. She was a big girl, athletic with a magnificent well-shaped body. Her legs were like sculpture; she was not slim, but she was well proportioned and even at the extraordinary height of six feet, she was womanly. Runia was proud of her daughter, especially when she took part in sport events. Tusia was a very good swimmer and a superb runner. Her physical education teacher had predicted that she would beat the record of the Polish women's running champion, Walasiewiczowna.

"Your daughter has all the qualities to become the next champion in running. She will bring a lot of pride to Poland.''

Runia smiled at the thought. She knew that for a Jewish girl to become a sport champion in Poland was difficult, but she didn't say a word at the time. Runia thought about her daughter and she was sorry that she could not pass for a Christian. Tusia was exceedingly beautiful but she looked Jewish. To look Jewish—Runia hated the expression—meant to have a somewhat dark complexion, dark hair, dark eyes and a quite prominent nose. The other day, Jozio, her son, told her,

"Mama—you are the only one in this family who could easily pass as a Christian.'' Jozio was seventeen years old. He was a very handsome boy. His whole face revealed his positive approach to life. He was always cheerful, smiling—and even in the worst moments (and they were happening often lately), Jozio was able to crack a joke. Yesterday evening, after Tusia left for a meeting (a very important one, she said) and Runia's husband, Morek, went to visit neighbors who considered themselves very well informed because they secretly listened to a radio program from England, Jozio asked his mother if she would hide a small gun for him.

"Please, don't ask anything of my father or Tusia," he said. Jozio didn't even ask for Runia's approval—he knew that his mother was always ready to do anything for him, no questions asked. In fact Runia loved her son more than anybody else in the world. He was the continuation of Runia's dreams—he had her way of seeing the world and people; he was gentle and loved life. Tusia and her father loved life also, but differently—they were less spontaneous, more reserved, less warm. And Runia needed warmth all the time—she had to be reassured constantly of the warmth around her.

I was lucky, Runia thought. I had more luck than wisdom because, really and truly, I didn't hide the two guns well.

She got up, took a chair and climbed onto it. On the topmost shelf in the small cupboard, just under the ceiling, the two revolvers lay in a corner. They were wrapped together in brown paper tied with ordinary string. The two SS men had taken everything from the dresser and from the large cupboard, but they hadn't touched this parcel. Runia smiled. She knew why. She got off the chair and took the long shawl in her hands. The package in which she had put the two revolvers had been covered with this shawl and it was this shawl which had caught the attention of the two SS men. They dragged it from the cupboard; and one of them said, "Look at these Jews—they were supposed to give the Germans all their furs long ago and here, see—they still have furs."

The second SS man took the shawl in his hand and said: "It's not really a fur and it's old. There are only some pieces of fur sewn together, the rest is knitted. This is a mixture of silk and fur."

The SS man laughed. "This shawl is yellow with age. I would not dare to send it to my *Edeltraut*."

Runia patted the shawl with affection and put it around her neck. She basked in its warmth. It was like going back in time and actually feeling the hands that had knitted the shawl with love.

Many years before, her aunt had sent her a beautifully wrapped package for her birthday. In it was this unusual shawl made of stripes of white ermine and ribbons of white knitted silk. Her aunt had knitted the fabric and a skilled furrier had put it together with the fur. In the letter enclosed with her gift, her aunt said that she had knitted two shawls, one white and one black. The black shawl she had sent to Lusia, the wife of Runia's older brother Jakub. Lusia had just entered the family of the Herzigs by marriage, and Runia's aunt wanted to "warm" Lusia with the gift.

Still wearing the shawl, Runia proceeded to put the room in order. She didn't want her family to see the mess. She was used to order—she liked order. It was the same aunt who had knitted the shawl who had taught her the beauty of order of long ago. She was more than an aunt to me, Runia thought. She was like a mother.

Runia had lost her real mother when she was only ten years old. Still, she remembered her well. Tenia Herzig was a good-looking woman, with a kind, round face, very long brown hair and brown eyes. As a child, Runia always admired her mother's hair styles—she kept changing them continually, and each time Runia thought that her mother was more beautiful. Her mother was never sick until the day she died. She had a miscarriage, a neighbor said. Runia didn't know what a miscarriage was and she only found out a day later that her mother was dead. Runia didn't want to believe it. No, it was not possible that she didn't have her mother anymore. How could she live without her?

Now in 1943, Runia still remembered her grief after so many years. She also remembered that her favorite time when her mother was alive was Saturday afternoon. Her mother would sit in the dining room and read. Her mother loved to read, but she never had time to do so during the week. Saturday was her only day for rest and reading. After lunch, Runia loved to sit near her mother and read with her. Runia would read children's stories and her mother would read novels or magazines and newspapers. She would prepare her reading matter on the prior Friday so that not a moment of her precious reading time would be lost. Runia recalled that on one of these Saturday afternoons her mother told her a story of her grandmother, her mother's mother. At the age of seventy-one, after her husband died, Runia's grandmother decided to emigrate to Palestine. Runia's mother described how the whole family tried to persuade her grandmother not to leave Stryj, the city in which she had lived her whole life, but nobody could change her grandmother's mind. The old lady, as she was called, bade good-bye to every-body and made the long journey all by herself. She lived afterwards for a few years in Palestine and died there alone but happy. This story of the courage of her mother's mother filled Runia with a warm pride.

When Runia's mother died, her brother Jakub remained with her father and Runia was taken to live with her aunt Rela. Runia had two older brothers, David and Herman, who were already at the university, but Jakub was only thirteen and still in high school. In spite of his age, he quickly became the man of the house. Runia's mother's death had thrown her father into a deep melancholy; in addition, he was in severe financial straits. Jakub started to work as a tutor to help his ill and depressed parent, who never recovered from his wife's untimely death. Runia was proud of Jakub who after finishing high school entered the university and became a lawyer as had his two older brothers.

Runia had now cleaned up the room. It looked as before. Everything was in order. The only difference was that she still had the shawl around her neck. She thought again about her old grandmother who had gone to Palestine. She was right. In Palestine nobody need be afraid if he or she looks Jewish.

Runia's heart started to beat faster. She wanted so much to protect her children and she didn't know how. The two revolvers were still lying in the cupboard. She tried to think of a safer place where she might put them. But none came to mind.

There was noise on the street. She went to the window. She saw a few youths surrounded by Gestapo men. She heard a shot. One of the Gestapo men fell, and the young people started to run in different directions. She heard many more shots. She stepped back from the window. She didn't want to see any more. She knew that many Jews would pay with their lives for the one life of the Gestapo man, but she felt no regret for what had happened.

Runia knew that on many occasions in the history of her people the time had come to fight for freedom and justice no matter the consequences. Now was the beginning of such a time. Tusia was right and Jozio was right. She decided to talk to her husband tonight. She wanted them to have a part in the resistance. She could show no less courage than her seventy-one-year-old grandmother who had voyaged to Palestine.

In time the noise on the street faded away.

A few minutes later Tusia came running in.

"Mama, Mama," she said, "did you hear? A short while ago a Gestapo man was shot. This is only the beginning."

Runia kissed her daughter. "How do you feel?"

"I feel fine," said Tusia. "I know that our days, even our hours, are numbered, but before I die, I will fight. I will fight together with the others. They will not take me like a sheep to the slaughter."

"Can I help you," asked Runia.

"Yes, you can. You are the only parent who knows that the Jewish resistance has started to receive arms. Tonight I will bring grenades here and a few more guns."

"How will you bring them?"

"I don't know how, but I have to meet Marcel in an hour and he will give me the instructions. I am not alone. Krzemieniec is becoming a very well organized city."

"Why so late? Why did we start to organize the resistance so late?" Runia asked.

Tusia looked at her mother.

"I was always so proud of you. Today I am even more proud. I thought that you only knew how to dream. Now I know you can also act—and fight."

Runia answered her daughter slowly:

"You don't know this because you are still very young, but the dreamers are the best fighters in the world. The dreamers dream about the blue sky, which belongs to every one. The dreamers need freedom to be able to dream."

When Tusia left, Runia took the shawl from her neck. She climbed on a chair and covered the package containing the two revolvers with the yellowing shawl of fur and silk—knitted with love.

*In memory of my cousin, Thea*
*(Tusia) Bross, daughter of Runia*
*Herzig-Bross and Maurycy Bross,*
*brother of Jozef Bross*

# The One-Hundred Meter Race

Tusia walked fast. She didn't want to lose even a minute. Her time was very precious today. The evening would be an important one. Her group was to meet, for the first time, the special Jewish emissary from Bialystok. The Jewish resistance, which had been growing in the last few months, was gaining ground, if not in a physical sense then in a moral sense. The Jews had decided to fight though they knew they had been abandoned by most of the world, starting with the powerful nations such as America and finishing with the nations who tried to retain their neutrality, such as the Swiss. She knew that the only neutral nation which would eventually try to help would be Sweden, but this was a drop in an ocean of suffering.

Jewish resistance, as Tusia saw it, combined a struggle for dignity with a sign to the world that Jews would not readily give up their lives. At this specific moment the struggle for dignity prevailed over physical survival simply because there were no gates open for life. Why was she thinking of "gates open for life?" It was the title of a poem she had heard only a few days before. How remarkable, thought Tusia, that people still write poetry. A poet is a dreamer like my mother. My father is a businessman—not a good one, maybe, but a businessman with a quite logical mind. I am like my father.

This train of thought, she realized, ensued from an exchange with her mother before she had left the house that day.

Her mother had said, "You look so pale today. Put on the pink sweater and put some lipstick on. You will look better, war or no war. Today you will meet the man you love. Try to look feminine."

Tusia laughed. "Who can think of looking pretty in times like these?"

"I can. You are young and to the man you love, you should be attractive."

"But, Mother, no one wears lipstick any more."

"It does not matter. At least, when you enter Marcel's room, you will give an impression of spring in the fall."

My God, Tusia thought, my mother is thinking of spring in the fall. But she put on the pink sweater and lipstick, after all.

Now, while passing the little streets, Tusia thought about Marcel. He was twenty-seven years old, as tall as she, handsome and strong. He had dark hair and very dark eyes. He had finished law school before the war. He was from Warsaw. He had lost his family the year before. He lived alone in a small room. Tusia thought that she spent the most important hours of her life in Marcel's room. Whenever she entered his room, she felt safe.

It was only a month before that she had fallen in love with Marcel. Before she had used to meet Marcel occasionally at a friend's house. She really didn't know how it happened that she fell in love.

One evening Marcel brought her home. Before the door of the apartment house where she lived with her family, he kissed her gently and said: "So many years I have waited for a girl like you." He caressed her hair and asked softly, "Have you ever been in love?"

"No," Tusia answered, "but now I am."

That evening became a turning point in Tusia's life. She could not explain why, but suddenly her existence took on a new meaning. She knew that Marcel had been involved with the Jewish resistance for several months. Now Tusia decided to get involved, to be with Marcel as much as possible. They didn't have much time to talk about themselves but even looking at each other was a comfort and a joy.

Marcel was often away on different missions, but she became used to waiting and hoping for his return. Sometimes she had to talk about Marcel. Jozio, her brother, teased her in the beginning but as he came to admire Marcel, he grew proud that Marcel loved his sister.

Tusia's parents approved of Marcel without hesitation.

"After the war you will have a good life together," her mother said. "I can see Marcel taking care of you, Tusia."

In Runia's voice was a certain sadness and Tusia thought she knew why. Tusia's father was a fine man. He considered himself a very good businessman. He represented a few big companies and traveled as a salesman. But he was never able to provide enough for his family, and Tusia's mother often did not know how to make ends meet.

Tusia's father was handsome, a brilliant talker in company, but he was essentially not a serious man. However, his relationship with Tusia was a special one. Morek cared for Tusia more than for anybody else in his family, and Tusia grew up as her father's pet. He still considered her, at twenty-one years old, his "little girl."

Only a few days before, she had been going home from work when she met her father on the street. Suddenly Morek asked her if she loved Marcel.

"Do you really love him?"

"I do," Tusia answered.

"Then, please, don't sleep with him until you marry him."

They did not discuss the matter any further because at that moment a neighbor happened by and all three walked home together.

Tusia had now reached Marcel's house. She entered it and ran up the stairs. She found the door of Marcel's room open. Marcel was standing in the middle of the room.

"God, how I waited for you today, Tusia. I needed you, I needed your warmth—at least for an hour or two. I wanted so much to be alone with you. Our meeting is an hour and a half away and during that time I want to feel you near me. I have never wanted you so much as today. Maybe it is because I am supposed to leave tomorrow on mission. But, then, we haven't had an hour alone together in the past two weeks."

Marcel took off Tusia's coat, her white woolen shawl, her white beret.

"You're lovely, Tusia. This pink sweater suits you so well—and you even have a trace of lipstick on your lips. My God, how good it is to see you this way."

Tusia smiled. "The pink sweater and lipstick were my mother's idea. She wanted me to look attractive to the man I love."

"I always thought that your mother was on my side, more than your father."

Marcel took Tusia in his arms. He held her tight.

"You will crush all my bones," Tusia said.

"Don't worry. You are a strong girl and I love your gorgeous body."

They lay down together on the couch. Marcel picked up Tusia's skirt. He looked at her legs in heavy stockings.

"Tusia, please take these ugly stockings off. I want to see your legs, kiss them, kiss all of you. You are my girl. I want you to be my woman now—today."

Tusia felt a warm thrill passing through her whole body. She looked at Marcel. His black eyes were shining, his hands were caressing her breasts now. His lips were kissing her ears. She felt Marcel's tongue in her ear. She got up. She took off her stockings, her sweater, her skirt. Marcel undressed himself completely. He uncovered his bed. Standing naked by his bed, Marcel seemed the embodiment of power and virility. Tusia was proud that this man wanted to be her first lover. Marcel unhooked Tusia's bra and took off her panties. She was standing now in full light, and she saw the admiration in Marcel's eyes.

"How beautiful you are," he said. He carried Tusia to bed in his arms. They lay still, caressing each other very gently. There was something beautiful in their restraint, as if they must first become acquainted with each other's body before they could be united. The war, the danger, was not present in the little room. Just two people in love engaged in the process of discovering each other. For a moment Tusia thought about her father's request that she not sleep with Marcel. But was this sleeping? Tusia was anticipating an unknown joy, and she was grateful to Marcel for not rushing her into it. Suddenly Marcel ceased his caresses. He looked into Tusia's eyes and whispered, ''I knew that you are beautiful, but I never expected such perfection. Your breasts, your legs, your arms are like sculpture. I love you, Tusia.''

Then Tusia felt Marcel's tongue between her lips. He opened her mouth and when his tongue touched hers, she felt a new delight and then Marcel moved his body over hers. Again they were still—almost not moving.

Marcel said: ''Do you want to belong to me?''

Tusia didn't answer. Marcel repeating, ''Do you want to belong to me?''

Tusia didn't answer.

Her whole upbringing came back at that moment. She had always thought of belonging to the man who would be her husband. She had looked forward to it. But Marcel was not her husband. Suddenly she was ashamed. As much as she wanted to belong to Marcel, she hesitated.

Marcel, sensing that something was wrong, moved off her. He was sitting on the edge of the bed now. There was sadness in his eyes, but Tusia was grateful for his understanding.

''Did I frighten you, Tusia?'' Marcel said. ''I hope I didn't. I never want to frighten you. I love you and I will always love you, and I can harness my passion if you wish because I love you so much. I don't want to hurt your feelings. I know the day will come when we will always be together, but I also want you to be mine only when you consent to be mine. You receiving me and I receiving you—not taking anything from you. My love is too holy.''

He took Tusia's head in his hands and caressed it gently. Now the caresses were different, purged of passion. Tusia wanted to say something, but she could not utter a word. She thought there was something wrong in not letting Marcel become her lover, but at the same time she knew that she was not ready—she wanted only more caresses, caresses. She needed to be more prepared—she was hungry for love, but she was afraid that once she belonged to Marcel, she would cease to exist for herself. There was something frantic in this retaining herself for herself; it frightened her.

Tusia put her head in Marcel's lap and started to talk.

''I need you, Marcel, I need you as a source of fresh spring water without which I don't want to live. I need you as a man and lover. But I am scared, scared of the hours passing by. I know that as long as I know that you love me, I can go on fighting and waiting for you but the moment our bodies become one, I will give up the fight. Please understand me.''

Tusia was crying now. She didn't know why, but she had to cry.

''Promise me that you will try to take care of yourself because I want you to make me a woman one day.''

''I promise,'' said Marcel. ''I will wait for the day when you will come to me, and I know that day will come.''

Marcel got up and looked at his watch.

"The meeting starts in twenty minutes," he said.

He returned to Tusia, kissed her breasts, her lips. Then he lay still in her arms for a few minutes.

"This was one of the most beautiful evenings of my life," Tusia said. She closed her eyes. She touched Marcel's face with her hand and she said: "I want my palm to remember the shape of your face."

Marcel kissed Tusia. "And I want my lips to remember the softness of your skin."

Tusia left the bed first. She dressed herself. Marcel buttoned Tusia's sweater. He smiled. "Do you know that I love you as much dressed as undressed —and I always will."

Tusia observed Marcel's movements. She felt sorry that they had to leave for the meeting.

The meeting took place in the apartment of a man named Roman. When Tusia and Marcel arrived, there were already ten people present.

"You are too late," said Roman to Marcel. "It never happened before. I will blame Tusia for it."

"Don't blame Tusia," said Marcel. "It was my fault—I wanted to spend a few minutes alone with Tusia. We are engaged. You can congratulate us."

Tusia was smiling. "I didn't know until now that this man is my fiance. However, I accept it. I am very happy."

Everybody was cheerful for a moment.

"Too bad we have nothing to drink," Roman said. "If I had known, I would have used my bartender's talent to prepare a special concoction. However, if not today, we will celebrate your engagement tomorrow, or another day."

The door opened. The Jewish emissary from Bialystok arrived. He was much younger than Tusia had expected him to be.

"My name is Tolek," the young man said.

Tusia looked at him closely now. She had seen him somewhere before—she was sure of it—but she didn't know where. He was slim and tall with blond, curly hair and blue eyes—he didn't look Jewish at all. Now the eyes of the young man met Tusia's eyes.

"Hello," he said. He approached Tusia. "Do you remember our meeting before the war in Poznan? You were on the girls' track team of your school and I was on the boys' team of mine."

Then Tusia recalled the day they met. She had lived in Poznan before the war.

"We met in a different time, in a different world," she said. "We were younger without worries and all that counted for me was the one-hundred meter race."

"I remember," Tolek said. "You won the race. The name of Tusia Bross was on every lip in my school."

"And you, you also won."

"Yes, but I only came in second. You won a gold medal but I only won a silver one."

Then the meeting was called to order.

The people present in Roman's room discussed the plans for getting arms, for making contact with the partisans in the forests and for maintaining communication among the various ghettos. The discussion lasted two hours. When it was over, Tolek told Tusia that he planned to stay another day in Krzemieniec and asked her if she would like to be the liaison between Krzemieniec and Bialystok. Marcel objected.

"I don't think," said Marcel, "that Tusia's looks are right."

"That may be so," Tolek said, "but Tusia is strong, she is a good runner. We need people like her."

In the end it was decided that Tusia would work within the ghetto in Krzemieniec. It was flattering to be singled out by the emissary from Bialystok but Tusia was glad to be near Marcel, and wait for him, when he was away, rather than be absent from the city.

Tusia and Marcel walked home together. They both had special passes which permitted them to be on the street after eight o'clock in the evening. They worked on different shifts in a shoe factory, and this enabled them to be abroad more hours of the day and night. At the corner of the street they were met by two policemen.

"What are you doing here?" a policeman asked.

"We are going to the shoe factory," said Marcel.

It was not true, but it was the only acceptable explanation of their presence in the street at this late hour of the night.

"You Jews," the policeman said, "you have no right to be here at night."

"Yes, we do," Marcel said. "We have special permits. We will show them to you if you wish."

"Come with us, you will show us these permits at the police post."

"Why at the police post?" Marcel asked.

Tusia knew that if they went to the police station, they would be arrested, because the police would easily find out that they were not scheduled to work in the factory tonight.

"Please let us show you our papers here," Tusia said.

In a very conciliatory voice she explained that they passed through this street very often and had never been stopped.

"You can go," said the policeman to Tusia, "but the man will go with us to the station."

"I will go with him," Tusia said.

"No," Marcel said. "Please go home."

Tusia hesitated, then walked on. She turned her head twice. The second time she saw Marcel running. There were shots. She saw Marcel entering a house. Now Tusia started to run. She sprinted up the stairs to her family's apartment. She woke up her mother. "Give me my gun," she said.

Runia got up. Without awakening anybody, she went to the cupboard. She climbed on the chair, unwrapped a parcel and handed Tusia the gun.

Tusia took the gun and raced out again. Nobody was on the street. She entered the house in which she expected to find Marcel. Marcel was not there. She stood in the doorway and looked up the street. Suddenly she saw Marcel. He was about 100 meters away. Two policemen were behind him. Tusia aimed the gun, then put it down. She could not kill. Suddenly an idea occurred to her and she bolted down the street. It would be the most important race in her life. She passed the two policemen. As she was handing the gun to Marcel, she heard a shot, then Marcel fired, then everything grew dim. She knew that she had won her race—but she did not know that this was the last race of her life.

*In memory of my cousin,*
*Igo Schoenfeld*

# The Locomotive

Igo was a tall, good-looking man with a lot of brown, wavy hair, dark brown eyes, and a dark complexion. There was something about him that inspired confidence. His handshake was firm, his arms were ready to embrace people, or to assist them in carrying something or to lift a child in the air and make him smile. Now Igo was rapidly climbing stairs. He wanted to reach the third floor as soon as possible because his sick friend, Leo, was waiting for him. In one hand Igo carried a small bag with half a loaf of bread and a jar of marmalade. In the other he held a bottle of milk. On the second landing, he was stopped by three children—two boys and one little girl.

"Mr. Igo, you promised last week to recite for us 'The Locomotive.' You promised, you promised."

The children were laughing and for a second Igo was transported into another world—the world before the war, when children were happy.

"I am sorry," he said, "I don't have time now. I will recite 'The Locomotive' for you tomorrow or another day. I have to see my friend Mr. Schleien, upstairs. He is all by himself and he is sick."

The little girl looked at Igo sadly and said:

"Please don't refuse us. Recite today. We don't know what will happen tomorrow."

Igo looked at the little girl who was maybe nine or ten years old, but wore the solemn expression of a grown-up. There was sorrow in her face, and fear looked out of her beautiful blue eyes.

Igo took the hand of the little girl in his and said, "All right. I will recite 'The Locomotive' for you today, but not now. First I must deliver this package and spend a few minutes with my friend. Come see me in half an hour upstairs. Then I will recite 'The Locomotive.' "

The three children clapped their hands and let Igo pass. He went upstairs. He had a key to his friend's apartment. Quietly he opened the door. First he went into the little kitchen and put the bag and bottle on a small table. The kitchen looked abandoned. There was no sign that somebody was using it. Since Leo's parents had been taken away, nobody cooked here.

Leo himself was too sick to cook. He had tuberculosis. A doctor who was visiting Leo regularly did not hold out any hope to Igo. "Leo needs a good sanatorium," the doctor told him, "a lot of care; you can't cure tuberculosis in the ghetto, even if you try. However, you can lighten your friend's life with your visits. They are important. Leo should not feel abandoned."

For some weeks, Igo shared the small apartment with his friend. He had moved here because he knew that the winter nights are long, that his presence would assure Leo that somebody in the world cared for him. Igo slept on a little couch in the so-called dining room. Although the Jews were very crowded in the ghetto and most people shared apartments, nobody wanted to move into Leo's place because Leo had tuberculosis.

It was strange how people were more afraid of contagious diseases than they were of bullets. A week ago Igo had seen a man shot on the street. That same man had discussed Leo's tuberculosis with him and advised Igo not to move into Leo's apartment.

Igo entered the room where Leo lay in bed. Leo's eyes were closed and he was breathing heavily. He was wearing Igo's blue pajamas, which were too big for him. Leo was very thin. His skin was white, almost transparent. He had long fingers. Leo's hands were delicate, like woman's hands. Igo regarded him from the door. He was not sure if Leo was asleep or not. If he was asleep, Igo didn't want to wake him. Leo opened his eyes. He tried to smile. Leo's blond hair was quite long and covered his forehead.

"How are you?" Igo asked.

"I am fine," Leo answered. As soon as he finished his sentence, he started to cough. When Leo coughed, his whole body shook. On Leo's lips Igo saw drops of blood. Leo wiped his lips with a handkerchief and lay still.

After a while he tried to make a joke.

"You see, as soon as I say that I am well, nature rebels and contradicts me—and reminds me that I am sick. Look, Igo, couldn't I pick up another illness. Nobody in my family has ever had tuberculosis before me, and nobody will have it after me."

The last words were said as if to himself.

"Let's face it," Leo continued, "after I die, there will be no more Schleiens. I am the last one."

"But you won't die yet. And I brought you a good piece of bread and marmalade and some real milk, not skim milk, but real milk, straight from the cow."

Leo smiled. "Where did you meet this cow?"

"I didn't meet the cow but I did meet an old friend of my mother in the marketplace. She came to the city to sell milk, and she let me have a half liter for you. I will warm it. It would be better if you drink the milk warm."

There was a knock on the door. "Who could it be?" Leo asked.

"It's the children who live on the second floor. I promised them I would recite them 'The Locomotive.' "

Igo answered the door. The three children looked up at him. "Fifteen minutes passed," said the little girl. "We are punctual. We went home, we watched the clock, and here we are."

"Please give me another ten minutes."

"Oh—all right," said the little girl. "We will wait for you on the stairs."

Igo closed the door; he went into the kitchen and warmed some milk. He poured it into a glass and put it on a tray. He also cut a slice of bread and spread some marmalade on it. He took a plate. The plate had a gold rim. This plate reminded Igo of evenings spent with Leo's family. He had often enjoyed the hospitality of his friend's home. Leo's parents had been well off. Everything in their home had been chosen carefully and was in good taste.

When Igo entered Leo's room with the tray, Leo said, "There is something else you could get for me."

"What is it?" Igo asked.

"If you would bring me some poison, I would never doubt your friendship."

"What are you saying? How could you even have such a thought?"

"Listen. Think about it. I know that the children are waiting for you. Please go, recite them the poem and after you finish, we can discuss my wish."

"I don't want to leave you now," Igo said.

"But you have to. The children are waiting for you. And anyway, you know very well that when I eat I cannot talk. If you want me to enjoy this delicious bread and marmalade and the milk straight from the cow, leave me alone for a while. Please go."

Igo left the room. Leo was right—it was better not to discuss the matter further now. Besides, Igo was shocked. He wanted to have a little bit of time for himself. However, he had to go downstairs and recite the poem for children.

How can I recite a poem, Igo thought, when my friend is asking me to give him poison?

From the next room, Igo heard Leo's voice.

"Igo, for what are you waiting? Please go downstairs and at least for a moment re-live the good old times."

Igo went back to Leo's room. Leo was smiling now. "Remember," he said, "how many children you have made happy in your life? Did you already forget how many schools you went to before the war and made Tuwim's poems popular? Even the most anti-Semitic teachers in Poland loved Tuwim's poems for children. Let's face it, Julian Tuwim, a Jew, gave something to Polish poetry that was unique. Tuwim was a magician with words and he knew how to transmit joy in simple forms. If you want to make me happy, please go downstairs now and recite not only Tuwim's 'The Locomotive,' but also 'The Birds' Radio.' So many children would want to hear you. Grab the occasion, Igo, and at least make these three children happy."

While going downstairs, Igo thought of the many times he had recited Julian

Tuwim's poetry. One of his favorite poems was "The Dancing Socrates," in which the wit and wisdom of the old Greek philosopher mingled. Igo had always admired Tuwim. There was something in Tuwim's poetry which was like the enchantment of a sorcerer—the way he could bring words together in order to strike, or caress, or to strike and caress at the same time. His love for the poet became Igo's profession. Before the war he had traveled from one city to another just to recite poems—not only Tuwim's but also those of other poets. He recited in winter and in spring, in small schools and big schools, sometimes during the day, sometimes in the evening. Igo didn't earn a lot. It was difficult to make ends meet. But Igo loved his work and he dreamed that one day he would organize a theater for poets. His parents did not approve of Igo's profession, but they didn't fight with him about it, either. His father used to say, "And one day the poetry will pass like a summer breeze." Now Igo's parents were dead and all he had left was the poetry—alone.

The three children were sitting on the steps. Igo stood beside them. "What would you like to hear?" he asked.

" 'The Locomotive,' " said the little girl.

"Do you know a poem called 'The Birds' Radio'?" Igo asked.

"Yes, I know," said one of the boys, "But I prefer 'The Locomotive.' "

"It will be best," said the little girl, "if today you recite 'The Locomotive,' and tomorrow 'The Birds' Radio.' That way we will have something nice to wait for tomorrow."

"It is nice," said one of the boys, "to wait for something good because now nobody expects anything good. Our parents talk only about terrible, terrible things."

Igo looked at the boy, who was perhaps ten or eleven years old. He wanted to take this boy in his arms and run somewhere far away—far from this ghetto, from this time, but Igo knew that there was no place to run to. Then he started to recite:

> *Stoi na stacji lokomotywa,*
> *czarna, ogromna i pot z niej*
> *splywa tlusta oliwa."*
> (There is standing at the station
> the locomotive, black, huge, and the sweat is
> pouring from her—the greasy oil.)

And Igo imitated the train. He articulated certain words in a special way, breathing fast or heavily, pronouncing sh-sh-sh- the way a train makes the sounds. The poem described a train full of people and animals. There were fat people who ate sausages and there were horses and there were bananas—everything was on this train and Igo mimicked the different things, as well as the locomotive running fast through the meadows and through the forest. The three children accompanied

Igo on this fantastic journey, their mouths open, their eyes shining.

Igo looked at the children and wished that the poem did not have an end.

When he finished, the little girl stood up and said: "Can I kiss you? I never kissed a great man and I think that you are great."

"Why do you think so?" asked Igo.

"Do you know why? Because you show people things not as they are, but as they could be. When you talk, the sky smiles, the rain becomes a white snow and snowflakes are dancing in the air."

"But I didn't say anything about the snowflakes dancing?"

"You don't have to. You teach people how to imagine. You also make people listen to the wind. I love poetry. Poetry is like a butterfly making the strings of the violin play."

Igo took the little girl in his arms. He felt her lips on his cheeks. Igo kissed her forehead and said:

"Tomorrow I will recite for you 'The Birds' Radio.' "

When Igo returned upstairs, Leo was asleep. He had eaten very little. On the tray was a half piece of bread and half a glass of milk. Leo seemed even paler than before. Igo observed his friend for a while, then looked out the window. The days are so short in November, thought Igo. It was dark outside. It started to rain and the drops of rain made Igo think of the music of time. The rain rhythmically touched the glass windows, first gently and then more insistently. After a while, it was hammering the window with powerful force.

Leo opened his eyes and said, "It is raining very hard. I was awakened by the rain. How did it go, your performance? Did the children like 'The Locomotive'?"

"Yes. Very much. And I promised them 'The Birds' Radio' tomorrow."

"Tomorrow? How do you know there will be tomorrow for us?"

Igo looked at Leo. He became frightened. He was thinking that Leo might have a high fever.

"How do you feel?" Igo asked.

"I feel very well," Leo asked, "and don't think that I have fever. I am lucid, more lucid than you think. I see what is going on around me."

Leo sat up. He seemed very agitated. "Because I don't believe in any tomorrow, Igo, please promise me that you will get the poison for me. I know a doctor who has potassium cyanide. You take it, you swallow it—that's all. Please, Igo, fulfill my deepest wish."

"I cannot. Your life is very precious for me."

"Is my life more precious to you than my wish?"

"Yes. I will not get you poison. Forget about it."

"Then promise me that when you see the immediate danger to yourself and the impossibility of taking care of me, you will try to help me finish my life."

"I cannot do such a thing. In life it happens sometimes that although we see danger near we are still not able to predict the outcome."

"But there is no outcome. There are no solutions to our situation." Leo was screaming now.

"Please calm yourself. Don't lose your strength. You are not too strong anyway."

"You see. You know I'm losing my strength and yet you refuse to help me die. Now, imagine, if today or tomorrow something happened to you, who would take care of me? No one. Listen to me—no one." Leo was spent now. He fell back on his pillows. Igo straightened them under his head. Leo closed his eyes again.

Igo didn't know how long he sat in the corner of the room. He listened to the rain for a while and then he thought about the little girl. She had said that he, Igo, was a great man because he knew how to recite children's poems.

Igo woke up. He had slept the whole night sitting on the chair in Leo's room. It was six o'clock in the morning. He had to get to work. But first he wanted to cook a few potatoes before going out. He went into the kitchen, washed himself and decided to change. He went to the dining room, where he kept his clothes. He took out fresh underwear and a clean shirt, and dressed himself fast. Then peeled the potatoes and put them on a gas burner.

Suddenly there was a knocking at the door. It was the man from downstairs, the father of the three children. He was crying. "I escaped," he said. "The SS men just took my wife and children—they are downstairs now. Run away if you don't want to be caught. They are taking people to the station. Nobody knows where they will go."

"I cannot run away," Igo said. "I have a friend here who is sick."

"Run away," the man repeated. Then he stopped crying and said: "Maybe you are right. You have to stay with your friend and I should join my wife and my children. We both have a responsibility."

Before Igo could say anything more, the man ran down the steps. Through the window in the dining room Igo saw a big truck full of people. The three children were standing beside the truck with their mother. After a while, the father joined them. They were all together now. There was another knock at the door. Igo opened it and saw two SS men.

They shouted, "Heraus, you have to go with us."

Igo tried to explain that he had a friend who was sick, but he was dragged and pushed to the stairs. There were other SS men on the steps. They surrounded Igo and took him downstairs.

An hour or so later, Igo was on the train, heading for he knew not where. When the train rounded a curve, Igo tried to see the locomotive. The sounds of the train were familiar to him. Again and again Tuwim's poem, which he had recited so many times, came back to him. The locomotive, the locomotive. There was something magical in the word. Igo could not think about anything else for a while, and he closed his eyes.

*In memory of my great-aunt,*
*Karolina (Karolcia) Hirsch-Rubel,*
*wife of Robert Rubel and*
*mother of four sons, Frydek,*
*Izek (Teddy), Mundek and Lonek*

# A Green Apple

K arolcia was peeling a green apple. She moved the knife around and around, as if she was playing with the skin, uncovering the whiteness of the apple slowly. It was important to her to peel the apple so that the skin came off in one piece, like a skewed ribbon. Since her childhood Karolcia had loved to peel apples this way. It was a skill she was proud of.

Karolcia's childhood was far, far off and it had been short because her parents died when she was very young and Karolcia married at the age of sixteen.

''It is wonderful to marry at sixteen, especially if you don't have parents,'' one of her aunts told her.

But Karolcia wasn't sure. And she had no one to ask if her aunt was right. Her younger sister, Tonia, certainly knew no more than she and her older brother was preoccupied with many family problems. But then, what choice did she have in the matter? Karolcia lived in Kolomyja, in eastern Poland, and the man chosen to be her husband, Robert Rubel, the son of the wealthy and respected Izak Rubel, lived in Jaslo, in western Poland. But the matchmaker had acted wisely. At the beginning of the marriage, Karolcia was a little fearful, but later she never regretted marrying so young and becoming Robert's wife. Robert was a quiet, good, warmhearted man and he tried to fulfill all her wishes.

Karolcia finished peeling her apple. She thought that when she had married Robert, she was like this green apple. Now after forty years, Karolcia thought that there are some apples which fall from the tree prematurely because of a very strong wind—some of them never become ripe but some of them when carefully put away, are allowed to ripen to maturity. Karolcia had been carefully sheltered and had thrived amid Robert's love and concern for her.

Karolcia was now sitting at the kitchen table, near the window. It was Friday. A few potatoes were boiling on the stove. Karolcia thought that the year 1943 was very difficult. The damn war, she thought. At the age of fifty-six she faced misery and hunger. Living in the ghetto in Kolomyja with her husband, she tried to cover the misery. But it was more difficult to cope with the hunger.

Robert was very weak. He needed better nourishment and Karolcia was unable to find this for him.

She thought about her home before the war, their beautiful apartment. They lived on the first floor in a house they owned. Their apartment had seven rooms. Six of the rooms were connected with one another, so that when the doors opened, it looked like one huge room, with a big mirror in the sixth room reflecting the first room in front. The first room was their everyday dining room; the second room was the bedroom of their two youngest sons, the twins, Lonek and Mundek; the third room was the master bedroom; the fourth room was her husband's study, the fifth room was a French salon; and the sixth room was a big dining room for special occasions. Behind this room, separate from the others, was the bedroom of their two older sons, Izek and Frydek. Karolcia saw in her mind all the rooms—one more beautiful than the others. Her husband's study was comfortable, with big armchairs covered in brown leather. The French salon was a real French salon with everything imported from Paris—the little chairs covered in a pink heavy brocade full of colorful flowers and *les rideaux*, the curtains made of a very fine French lace, beside which the drapes of pink velours looked like something from a fairy tale castle. The dining room for special occasions was paneled in dark wood and the chairs were covered in Karolcia's favorite color, blue. How many wonderful evenings had Karolcia spent there!

I am not old, she thought. I feel strong and full of life but when I look around, I realize that life is slipping away. Every day the number of victims grows, every day there are fewer among us.

She thought of her sons now. She was always pleased when people asked her, "How many children do you have?" because she could answer with pride: "I have four sons." To be the mother of four strong, young men was, for her, the greatest gift of destiny.

When the boys were young, one neighbor used to say, "Take care of them. They are all so good looking—beware of the evil eye."

But Karolcia was not superstitious. She did not believe in an evil eye. She believed in God—it was to God that she was always directing her thoughts, and her thoughts were like prayers. She never really prayed except on the High Holidays in the synagogue. It was her husband who prayed at home every day. Karolcia thought that by bringing up a fine family, she prayed with her deeds, that by providing her family with a beautiful and happy home, she praised God. If man was made in the image of God, God wanted every man to have a happy home. Man's home should be like God's which is heaven, Karolcia believed.

But now her home was nothing like heaven. She looked at the few green apples on a plate in the middle of the table and thought. In our former home there was always something ready for the unexpected guest, but here, if somebody came, I would have only green apples. She took the knife and cut a quarter from the apple she had peeled. She bit the slice and thought. Sour—very sour, but better than nothing. How many times had she said in her mind, "better than nothing.'' The thought made her angry. She had always sought quality in her life and now . . . But she must not dwell too much on her past.

Karolcia got up and cleared the table. She opened the drawer of a little dresser and took out a white tablecloth. She covered the table and she put in the middle of it a small plate on which, for many months, she had been lighting her Friday night candles. She used the plate because her candlesticks had been taken by the Germans immediately after their arrival in Kolomyja. Karolcia looked at the white tablecloth and thought that even if the candlesticks had disappeared, the Friday night spirit would never leave her home. That was her victory over Hitler.

The door opened. Robert entered the kitchen. He was a pale-faced man, grey haired and bent beyond his years. He watched Karolcia preparing the Sabbath table. She was a beautiful woman, tall and majestic like a queen. She was wearing a long housecoat which accentuated her height. Her short-cut blond hair which was beginning to grey, shone in the afternoon sun. Karolcia's face was very expressive; her blue eyes still had a youthful look.

As she turned to him, Robert said,

''Anytime I see you, I thank God that He gave you to me as my wife.''

Karolcia smiled. She said: ''I haven't heard anything like this from you in many years. Why are you now paying me a compliment?''

''When I see you standing there and the rays of the sun shine in your blonde hair, I think that through all the years we spent together I have admired you for something else every day. One day I admired the way you combed your hair; one day I admired the way you raised our boys. There was always something special in you that I admired, and each morning I have thanked God for you.''

Karolcia started to laugh. ''And I have to wait until today to hear this?''

Robert suddenly became serious. ''Better late than never—and I think it is now very, very late. Our days are numbered. I do not believe that we will survive much longer.''

Robert took a chair. Karolcia remained standing.

''Sit down—please,'' he said. When Karolcia was seated he spoke again.

''There are rumors that all the Jews in Kolomyja will be deported.''

''What do you mean?''

''Yes, apparently we will be deported to various labor camps.''

''I don't believe it. We live in an age of rumors, of false information. Who told you, Robert?''

''Ania, the young woman who works in the store. She is Polish but her friend is German and this German told her that all Jews will have to leave Kolomyja.''

''I don't believe it,'' Karolcia said again.

Now Robert got up. He took off his coat and from its pocket removed a small bag of flour.

''Take this, Karolcia, and bake something if you wish. Today is Friday.''

Karolcia opened the bag and exclaimed, "This flour is almost white! Where did you get it?"

"I met your brother on the street. He gave it to me."

Karolcia looked at the flour again and said:

"My brother always thinks of me—at any time and place."

Robert turned to the little room which served as their bedroom.

"I will lie down. Somehow I don't feel too strong today. It must be the flu that took the rest of my strength."

"Yes, rest," said Karolcia. She went into the room, puffed up the pillows, and prepared the bed.

"You lie down and I will prepare our evening meal. War or no war, Friday night should be Friday night as long as we are free."

Robert repeated, "As long as we are free. What will be tomorrow, no one knows."

"Tomorrow we will have enough time to think about it, tomorrow."

"How things have changed," Robert said, "that now I don't recognize you. Before the war you always wanted to think about tomorrow. You tried to foresee situations, to build our future, and now you don't even want to talk about tomorrow."

"Yes, it is true. Because before the war we were able to think of how to act in more or less normal, predictable situations. Now we have only two possibilities—to run away, and we don't know where, or to stay and not preoccupy ourselves with problems we cannot solve. Please, Robert, lie down and try to regain a little bit of your strength."

Robert didn't say a word. When Karolcia had covered him with a blanket, he closed his eyes. Karolcia went back to the kitchen.

She decided to make a small challah from the flour that Robert had brought to her. She would even use the eggs and some saccharin to make the challah sweet. She wanted this challah to be better than any she had baked before, because she felt that this would be their last Friday night here. A few days before she had heard the same rumor as Robert: that all the Jews would be taken somewhere. But the challah should be tasty.

She started to think of her four sons. Where are they? Karolcia thought.

Lonek, the youngest, was in Lwow. His twin, Mundek, had been taken by the Russians to Siberia. Her second oldest, Izek, was studying medicine in Italy, and Frydek, the oldest, who was an engineer, was in Rumania. She was almost happy that three of her sons were out of Poland.

They will survive, she repeated to herself like an incantation. But what about Lonek in Lwow? Lonek is strong, tall, blond with blue eyes—he will also survive. Karolcia was baking the challah now, in a special pot because she didn't have any baking dish. She looked at the small, braided bread and she thought about her youngest son.

Suddenly, somebody knocked at the door. It was a mailman. The letter was postmarked Lwow. My God, Karolcia thought. It must be from Lonek. There was no sender's name on the envelope. Before opening the letter, Karolcia looked into the other room. Robert was sleeping. She closed the door and read the letter. It was from a friend of Lonek and it said that Lonek had been taken to the Janowska camp in Lwow.

Karolcia read the letter again and again as in a daze. The friend of Lonek didn't give any address. He wrote that he would contact her again. But Karolcia, still looking at the letter, decided she must act immediately.

She wrote a brief note to her husband and left it near the door. She took the challah from the oven. She changed, put on dress and coat and ran outside. As she hurried down the street she took off her armband with the Star of David. With her blonde hair and blue eyes, she would be safer without it since she was going to a part of the city where Jews were forbidden to live. There she had an old friend, a Polish woman whose sons were in the underground. She would give the woman money to help her son in the camp. She knew that the Polish underground organization had the ability to bribe Germans. But first she had to sell her watch. She knocked on a familiar door.

The door opened and an older woman let Karolcia in. "Come in, come in," she said with a smile. Karolcia entered and laid a gold watch on the table.

"I need money," Karolcia said.

"Don't sell it," said the woman. "I know that this is your last piece of jewelry. Maybe you will need it tomorrow."

"No, no," said Karolcia, "I need money now."

"Why?"

"Because my son is in the Janowska camp in Lwow."

"What will you do with the money?"

"I will give it to somebody who will try to bribe the German authorities. I have to help my son."

The woman gave Karolcia 300 *zlotys*. Karolcia thanked her. She was glad that the transaction hadn't taken much time.

Now Karolcia passed another street and entered an apartment house. There she spoke to her Polish friend whose sons were in the underground. The woman promised to contact her sons immediately. When Karolcia handed her 300 *zlotys,* the woman hesitated.

"Maybe this is your last money. Don't give everything away."

"I have to, I have to. I am a mother and my son needs help."

The woman said that in a day or two she would come to see Karolcia even if it became difficult. Thanking her, Karolcia left. She walked fast. She hoped that Robert was still asleep. She didn't want to tell him about Lonek.

Robert was asleep. Karolcia put the challah back in the oven, and she waited now. She didn't have anything else for this Sabbath meal except a few potatoes and some marmalade. She could not think of anything but her son.

Twilight came, grey, November twilight.

Karolcia summoned Robert. She cut one candle into two halves and lit the halves. Robert in his black yarmulka, looked tired in spite of his sleep. He watched her as she recited the Sabbath evening prayer.

Suddenly there was a knock on the door. It was a Jewish policeman. "Mrs. Rubel," he said, "we need some jewelry. The German authorities want jewelry from the Jews. Maybe this way we will postpone the deportation."

"I don't have any jewelry," Karolcia said. Robert looked at her. She knew that he was thinking about her watch. "I don't have any jewelry," she repeated.

"How is it," asked the Jewish policeman," that such rich people don't have anything?"

"I sold everything," said Karolcia.

When the policeman left, Robert asked Karolcia why she didn't give him her watch.

"We are in danger," Robert said, "and you refused to give up your watch. What are you doing?"

Karolcia didn't answer.

"Tell me the truth. Why didn't you give him you your watch? Please tell me the truth."

"I am sorry, but it is the last piece of jewelry I possess. You gave it to me when our twins Lonek and Mundek were born. It has shown me many happy hours and I cannot part with it. One watch more or less will not make any difference. Now, let's make a blessing. Our supper is ready."

The door burst open. Two SS men came in. One threw the challah on the floor and the other extinguished the two candles. "The Jews don't need Friday nights anymore. *Heraus, heraus*—take your coats and come with us.

When Robert put on his coat, he whispered to Karolcia, "I am so happy that you kept this watch which I gave you. You were right."

*In memory of my cousin,*
*Jadwiga (Jadzia) Rosenfeld,*
*daughter of Hania Rosenfeld*
*and granddaughter of*
*Huny and Siandzia Rubel*

# Solo

Jadzia possessed very special looks. There was something almost mysterious in her green eyes, her very light skin, and her auburn hair. A few freckles on her nose accentuated her beauty with flecks of tawny gold. Jadzia adored the color green, all shades of green. She was always very elegant. Her mother had spoiled her since childhood. Jadzia had lost her father, a medical doctor, during the First World War when she was two years old. To make up for that her mother had tried to give her everything—the best and the most beautiful.

When she was a teenaged girl Jadzia was ready to fall in love. She missed her father tremendously. It was as if she could never have enough love at home. She lived with her mother, her grandparents and an uncle. They were all kind to her but she longed for something else, something more.

Jadzia's favorite occupation was to play piano. She played beautifully, and at the age of eighteen, after finishing high school, she went to the music conservatory in Krakow. She was very talented and was graduated with honors. After finishing her studies, Jadzia thought of becoming a concert pianist, but she fell in love with a young man and decided just to teach. She didn't want to be separated for too long from her friend.

Her mother did not approve of Jadzia's choice. The young man was German. "Germans and Jews in 1937—this does not make any sense," said her mother. It was true that Hans was not a Nazi but he was German. After one year of engagement, Jadzia decided to break up with her fiance, and she came back from Krakow to Jaslo, back to her mother and her grandparents.

She immediately became a very popular teacher. She had many students and she was good at showing off the accomplishments of her students. Jadzia added a spark of life to any company, and the little town of Jaslo appreciated her very much. Jadzia was fun and people liked her. In January, 1939, she met an intelligent young man, a Jew from Sosnowiec, and married him in September at the beginning of the war. She was happy to marry Walter, a big, tall, beautiful man. "My giant," Jadzia would call her husband, "my Jewish giant."

Walter was very strong, but he was also gentle and kind. And he loved

Jadzia more than anything in the whole world. "If somebody would offer me a star in the sky and ask me to leave Jadzia for a month, I would refuse the star," he once said.

But now Walter was in a labor camp and Jadzia was all alone. Her grandparents had been killed some time ago and her mother taken by Germans a week before—only she was left.

Jadzia sat on the bed in the tiny room in which she had lived with Walter. She was wearing a green skirt and green sweater. In a corner was her little suitcase, packed with enough for several days. She wanted to run away but she didn't know where to. There were only a few other Jews left in Jaslo. Jadzia knew that in another day or two everybody would be taken somewhere.

Suddenly she heard some noise on the street. It was five o'clock of a dark December evening, but as she looked through the window, she could see the truck and the SS men. She decided to act fast. She would go through the kitchen and take the back door steps leading to the backyard. She was not sure if she could reach the backyard without being spotted, but she knew that this was her only chance. She took her purse and decided to leave the suitcase. She ran down the steps from the back door. She didn't see anybody in the backyard. She ran through the backyard. She found herself on a deserted street. She didn't want to look back. She wasn't wearing her Star of David. In her haste, she had taken only a green jacket instead of a coat. Now, on the street, Jadzia was cold. The wind was strong and was pushing against her. The streets were almost deserted. Suddenly Jadzia heard some footsteps and ran until she came to the Sokol Building which served as a movie theater in Jaslo. She knew the building from having played piano there in the past.

The main door was locked. Jadzia decided to try the back door. The back door was not locked.

She entered the theater. It was dark. In darkness she tried to find her way to the stage. She knew the stage well. Finally she was on the stage. She remembered where to look for the switches. She turned on the lights. On the stage was a piano, the same piano on which Jadzia had played so many times. She decided she would spend the night here.

Jadzia hadn't had a piano for almost two years. One day a German officer had come to their home, complimented her on her piano and the next day the piano was removed from her house. Now the piano in the theater awoke many memories. It was a beautiful concert Bechstein, and she thought that, even if it was for the last time in her life, she would play it again.

But the piano was locked. She opened her purse, shook out some coins, a little sapphire ring of her mother's, a mirror, a lipstick and a knife. She tried to open the piano with the knife. But the blade was too wide; it would not go into the narrow keyhole. She was almost in despair when she spotted the key. It lay on a far corner of the piano. She put the knife back in her purse. She opened the piano with the key and sat down on the bench.

After removing her jacket, she put her hands together as she always used to do before a concert and started to play. She didn't know why, but she was playing Schubert's "Ave Maria." She remembered that once she had been asked to improvise on the theme of "Ave Maria." Now she was doing the same thing. The Jewish woman Jadzia was playing "Ave Maria" as a cry of one Jewish woman to another. Maria had been Jewish as was her son Jesus. Jadzia didn't know why, but while playing, all these thoughts mingled in her mind.

After a while, she stopped. She decided to play themes from Prokofiev's opera, *The Love of Three Oranges*. Again she improvised and while playing she visualized oranges—millions of oranges. Jadzia thought she heard some footsteps. She stopped playing, listened. Nothing. She began a concerto of Prokofiev, a concerto for the left hand. No improvising now. She wanted to prove to herself that she had not forgotten. The cascade of smooth sounds vibrated. Jadzia forgot the war, the danger. She was playing now, solo, solo.

Through Jadzia's mind memories of yesterday were now passing. Her German fiance, her husband, her mother, her first music teacher, Mr. Mirski, who would say, "Play, my little one. The greatest treasure of man is his music."

And he was right, Jadzia thought. Even now, facing death, I can enjoy music. Jadzia stopped for a while. About whom else had she to think? Her grandparents were dead; her mother was dead; her husband was in the labor camp. Her relatives were far away, she was alone. No, Jadzia thought. Prokofiev is with me, and Schubert, and . . . Chopin. How was it, that she hadn't yet played Chopin? Chopin was her greatest hero. Slowly as if she were touching the holy tones, she started to play E Minor Concerto. She was wandering with Chopin through the Polish fields and along the Vistula. She thought about Paris and Majorca, about George Sand, and about Chopin dying young. Jadzia had to play. She didn't care anymore if somebody heard her; she didn't care if she would die tomorrow. For the last time Jadzia wanted to play—solo, solo.

Jadzia didn't know how long she played. She stopped for a while. She was cold. She put on her jacket. Her movements were not as free as before, but she continued to play. When she started to play the Polonaise in A Major, she thought that she had completely overcome her fear. Chopin gave her an unusual strength. She was not cold anymore. She stopped playing. She took off her jacket and she started again to play the Polonaise in A Major from the beginning with mysterious force. Who are Germans? she thought. Who is Hitler? Hitler is a coward who is afraid of Jews. He is obsessed with Jews because deep in his mind he doesn't believe he can ever destroy them. And his killers are the greatest cowards because they are afraid to face living people. A brave man can stand up for his beliefs without killing.

Now playing the Polonaise in A Minor, Jadzia was not cold anymore; she was not hungry. She played as if in ecstasy. It was her prayer of thankfulness to God for music, for Schubert, for Prokofiev, for Chopin. She didn't ask for anything in her prayer, she only thanked God for the playing. She now remembered that her father who died very young, loved music. This also had a special meaning for her now. It meant that nothing disappears in life. Her father had implanted the love of music in her and she had implanted that love in her pupils. Jadzia thought about her pupils now, Renata Cukier, Rena Herzig, and so many others. They would never forget music. And even if ʳʰᵉ died, some of her students would survive and remember what she had taught them.

Jadzia played solo in the Sokol Theater: Chopin for the world, Chopin for her husband, Chopin for her father who had died years, years before. She also thought that she played for all those who were on the battlefields, and who didn't want to fight, and who didn't want to kill. She didn't want to believe that all the soldiers wanted to kill. She didn't want to believe it. She wanted to believe that they would rather listen to music than fight. She was sorry that she had never asked any soldier if he preferred music or fighting. No, Jadzia knew that people loved music. And there, on the battlefields, was only the music of cannons and of dying hearts, which were stopping their rhythmic beats.

When she finished she heard applause. She turned her head and she saw a young, tall SS man. Still clapping, he said in German, "Marvelous playing. You played for me and now I will play for you."

The SS man strode toward Jadzia. She decided to try to escape. The stage in the theater was quite large, the piano in the middle of it. Jadzia took her purse and ran toward the door. The door was locked.

"I have the key," said the SS man.

They were both running now around the piano.

"Open the door," Jadzia said.

"If you stop running, I will open the door."

The SS man opened the door, then locked it again. This time he left the key in the door. He came back. Finally he grabbed Jadzia. He held her and started to kiss her. He began to tear off her clothes. Jadzia understood that he wanted to rape her. She was fighting, clawing, she scratched his face. But when he wanted to pull her skirt down, she opened her handbag. She took out the knife and stabbed the SS man in the chest. He gasped, "let go," and fell to the floor. Jadzia ran to the door. She went outside. It was cold but she was free.

*In memory of my cousin,*
*Stefan (Stefus) Eibschutz, son of*
*Hela Rubel-Eibschutz and grand-*
*son of Leon and Goldzia Rubel*

# The Little Don Quixote

S tefus was nine years old. He looked eleven or twelve. He resembled his uncle Mundek, his mother's brother, whom he admired. Stefus was built like a wrestler ready to enter the ring.

One day he overheard a German policeman say:

"Look at the little Jew—he must be very strong."

Stefus pretended he didn't hear or understand the words of the German, but he was proud of his appearance. He not only looked strong, he was strong. All the children in the street knew this, but they also knew that Stefus would never provoke a fight.

Stefus lived with his mother in his grandparents' house. His parents were divorced. He really didn't know his father. He had seen him when he was very young, once or twice before the war. Some father, Stefus would think. He doesn't care to get to know me better. There was anger in the child when he thought of his father, but he knew how to console himself immediately. Instead of his father, he had his grandfather, his grandmother, his mother and uncle Mundek. His uncle was very, very tall and very strong. He was also good looking. Women would say this even in front of Stefus. Uncle Mundek was Stefus' idol. Stefus loved to listen to his uncle. He told him stories about places in different distant lands. Uncle Mundek had spent many years in Belgium and in Holland, and he often talked to Stefus about the tulips and windmills and the canals. Stefus was especially fascinated by the windmills.

Stefus' mother, Hela, was a short, thin woman with a very expressive small face and big black eyes. Stefus did not resemble her at all. When he was four years old, he told her:

"I am strong and I will protect you."

His mother was very proud of his words. The whole family soon knew about them. At first Stefus was not too happy about this, but he nevertheless intended to keep his promise. Once, before the war, when his mother was sick, he took care of her a whole day when his grandmother had to make a journey from Jaslo to Rzeszow.

Before the war, Stefus lived in Jaslo, in western Poland. At the beginning of the war the whole family fled to Lwow. There they stayed in Mundek's home. Mundek was already married to a very plump lady.

During the first two years of the Russian occupation, Stefus attended school. He had to learn Russian and Ukrainian. He didn't mind—he liked to learn. His uncle told him that learning is like opening the gates of the world. Life in Lwow at the beginning of the war was not as pleasant as it had been in Jaslo, but Stefus got used to his new surroundings. One day, when he came home from school at the beginning of 1941, he found his grandmother lying on the floor in the kitchen. Sha had had a heart attack and she died. Somebody in the family said that she died from a broken heart, that she could not live in a home that was not hers.

Whatever the cause, it was difficult for Stefus to comprehend his grandmother's death. He knew that people were dying, but it was the first time he had experienced the loss of someone he loved. Goldzia Rubel had a round, smiling face; she was always full of the joy of life; and seeing her lying on the kitchen floor, dead, made a very great impression on Stefus. "Why? Why? Why?" he asked his mother, his grandfather, his uncle. And nobody could answer him.

For several days Stefus cried. He didn't know why he cried, but one night he understood—he didn't want anybody to die. All this was when the Russians were in the city. Then people were often taken to prison or to camps in Russia, but nobody he knew died, except his dear grandmother.

When the Germans came, everything changed in Lwow. There was not a day anymore when somebody he knew or was related to didn't die. And Stefus didn't ask why anymore. He knew that the Germans didn't like Jews and therefore they killed them.

One day he asked his Uncle Mundek:

"Do all Germans hate Jews?"

His uncle answered the question with a question.

"Why are you asking?"

"Because I don't believe that all, all the Germans hate Jews. Some have to be good. When I was very small, my grandmother told me that in every nation there were good and bad people."

"Bad or not bad," Uncle Mundek said, "they kill Jews just the same. Some of them say that they are obeying orders."

"Do people have to obey such orders?"

His uncle didn't answer this question and soon they were talking about Holland.

But the question came back to his mind again when a man he knew approached him on the street and asked if he would like to help in beating up the Germans. The man's name was Roman; he was a brother of Krysia, with whom Stefus played sometimes in the backyard of their home. Krysia was nine years old, the same age as Stefus, but her brother was a grown-up seventeen-year-old.

"How can we beat up Germans?" Stefus asked Roman.

"I will show you one day," Roman answered, "but under one condition—that you will keep our secret. Nobody has to know about our conversation. Even my sister Krysia."

"She is a girl," Stefus said. "I understand. Fighting is for men, not for girls."

Roman did not answer, but a day later Stefus met him again and this time Roman gave him a small envelope and asked him to deliver it to Sloneczna 12. Sloneczna Street was quite long. Stefus had to go far. However, he delivered the letter.

He came home late and his mother was worried.

"Where have you been?" she asked.

"I was playing," Stefus said. This was the first time in his life he had lied to his mother. But he thought he was right. The letter was a secret between Roman and him.

Late in the evening his Uncle Mundek asked Stefus to come to his room. When Stefus did so, his uncle closed the door. Then he asked Stefus what he had been doing on Sloneczna 12. At first Stefus wouldn't answer, but Mundek insisted, and after a while Stefus admitted that he had delivered a letter given him by Roman.

"Do you know what was written in the letter?"

"No, I don't know," Stefus answered.

"But I know," said Mundek. "There is an organization now which has decided to fight the Germans—the time has come when we have to fight. Do you know about it?"

"No," said Stefus, "but I think they are right. My grandmother died because she had a heart attack, but now people die because the Germans think that there is not enough room in the world for them and the Jews. I want to fight too."

"Wait," Mundek said. "Wait. One day I will talk to you about it, but not today."

"Why not today? I want to talk now."

"Listen," said Mundek. "I have to think about it. Let me tell you today the story about Holland, a country which I love very much—I promise you that today we will talk about Holland and tomorrow we will talk about fighting the Germans."

Mundek and Stefus were talking about the tulips and hyacinths of Holland, about millions of flowers sold in big and small markets all around the country. They also talked about the windmills, about Amsterdam and the Dutch people.

"The Dutch people," said Mundek, "they don't hate Jews like the majority of the Poles and the Ukrainians do. I believe that after the war we will find that the Dutch people had helped the Jews during the trying times. Here it is different—

we have to fight the Germans but at the same time we have to be very careful with the Polish and Ukrainian population—they dislike us also.''

"But there are also good Poles and good Ukrainians," said the child. "I remember my grandmother taught me that among all people are good and bad."

There was something in the voice of Stefus that captured the attention of Mundek. Suddenly the adult understood—the child did not believe that all the Poles or all the Ukrainians or all the Germans were bad. Mundek also understood that he didn't have any right to dwell on it—because if, in spite of the war, the child preserved the notion of people being good, he had no right to take it away from him.

At that point Stefus' mother came in, interrupted them and said that it was time for Stefus to go to bed.

The next morning Stefus got up very early. He could not sleep. He was anxious to talk to Roman or to Mundek about fighting the Germans. He wanted to help. Unfortunately, his uncle had already gone out, so Stefus went looking for Roman.

Roman was at home. Again he handed something to Stefus. This time it was a bigger package.

"I have to know what is inside," said the child.

"All right," Roman said. "I will tell you, but promise me you will not talk about it to anybody."

"I promise."

"In this package are plans of the city of Lwow. You will take them to the same place you went before. But be careful. If somebody catches you, just say that you found the package on the street."

"I want to know more."

"I cannot tell you more."

Stefus left for Sloneczna 12 immediately. He held the package under his jacket. First he ran, but then he decided it was better just to walk fast. Two German soldiers passed him—they were laughing. Later, he saw an SS man coming down the street. He changed sides of the street; he didn't want to pass the SS man. After he crossed the street he heard some noise. The SS man was beating two Jewish men who were carrying suitcases.

Stefus went into the front door of a building. He wanted to see what the SS man would do to the two men. The SS man took the two suitcases, opened them, and threw their contents on the pavement.

"Jewish garbage!" he screamed. "Where were you going? You should be working now."

The two men tried to explain something; Stefus didn't hear their words. After a while, the SS man took the two men off. The open suitcases and all their strewn contents were left on the street.

Stefus forgot about his package. He wanted to pick up the suitcases, put the clothing back in and return them to the men. His package fell. Now Stefus was ashamed. How could he forget? He didn't have any right to stop for the suitcases. He remembered hearing his uncle say that many people lost their lives because they couldn't part with their belongings. He picked up the package and went on his way. When he reached Sloneczna Street, he saw a truck full of SS men. At first he intended to pass them and enter Number 12 but then he thought that, order or no order, it was better not to go inside.

He went back home. His mother asked him where he had been. He didn't answer. She asked him to take his jacket off. Stefus said he didn't want to.

"I am cold," he said.

"Oh, my God," Hela said. "You've caught cold. Let me take your temperature."

"I don't want your thermometer," said the boy.

"Then why do you want to keep your jacket on?"

He tried to hide the parcel, but his mother saw it. She reached into his jacket and took it out. There were maps of Lwow, marked with red Xs where the German posts were situated.

"Who gave you this package?"

Stefus didn't answer.

"Who gave you this package?" she repeated.

"No one."

"Who gave you this package?" she said again.

Stefus didn't answer. He shook his head. Hela slapped her son's face very hard.

"You will answer me," she said, "and if not, I will slap you again."

"Slap me as many times as you want," Stefus cried. "I will not tell you who gave me this package."

The door opened. Mundek came in. "What is going on?" he asked.

"Look at him," Hela said. "We don't have enough problems—he wants to give us additional ones. Look at all these maps with the German posts in Lwow. Look!"

Mundek folded the maps and put them together.

"I will take care of this," he said.

"What? You will take care of this? Are you saying you approve of Stefus' behavior."

"I don't approve of Stefus' behavior but I approve of the behavior of people who want to fight Germans. Listen. Just a little while ago they arrested fifteen young men on Sloneczna 12."

"Oh, my God," Stefus spoke. "I was supposed to go there. I was supposed to bring them the maps. Maybe they needed these maps."

"What?" his mother said. "You were supposed to go there?"

"Yes. I want to fight."

"You see," his mother turned to her brother. "This is what happens when

Stefus spends a lot of time with you, Mundek. You talk to him about windmills and then he wants to fight.''

"What are you talking about?'' asked Mundek.

"To fight with Germans is like fighting with the windmills—in Holland or in Spain. My brother and my son are two Don Quixotes, only bigger and not so thin. Don Quixotes.''

At that moment Stefus' grandfather came in and Hela fell silent.

Late that night, Stefus talked to Mundek. He asked his uncle about Don Quixote; he wanted to know who Don Quixote was. Mundek tried to explain as best he could. He spoke about the creator of Don Quixote, the author Miguel de Cervantes Saavedra, who lived in Spain. Mundek described Don Quixote as a knight of spirit who tried to see the world as beautiful and just. Mundek talked also about Don Quixote's Sancho Panza, who tried to teach reality to Don Quixote.

Stefus didn't understand much of what Mundek said, especially when he talked about fighting with the windmills. Stefus thought windmills were fascinating.

"I don't mind fighting with the windmills,'' Stefus thought. "First, maybe I will fight with the windmills, but later on I will try to make the world a better place to live. I am nine years old, but I am a man. The time of good people is not gone. My grandmother was right—there are many good people in the world.''

"It is late,'' Mundek said. "You had better go to sleep.''

"Please let me stay up a while,'' said the boy. "I want to hear more about Don Quixote.''

It took Mundek a few minutes to explain to Stefus what a knight-errant was. At the end of the conversation, Stefus concluded that Don Quixote was a good man, but he didn't fight enough.

"I want to fight, I want to fight,'' he repeated.

That night Stefus had a dream. He was Don Quixote, but he didn't wander through Spain, he wandered through Lwow. He went to all the German posts which were indicated on his map, and at every post he saw a windmill. He didn't know what to do. Instead of Germans there were windmills, turning, turning.

**STORIES BY JAKUB HERZIG**

# The Hasidic Dance

## I

I was very familiar with the town of Dabrowa, near Tarnow. The first time I arrived there from Eastern Galicia was at the end of 1910. Dabrowa had 4,000 inhabitants, 60% of them Jews.

This was an interesting Jewish population. They were good, agile workers, skilled businessmen, exporters of different kinds of merchandise out of the country. In town there were Jews who had their workshops, small factories—you could not find there any lazy people. They were the Hasidim, with long beards and earlocks, wearing long *capotas*. They lived together in harmony and mutual trust with Poles. They were respected. The director of the District Bank was a Jew, and according to tradition, the assistant to the mayor was always a Jew. Among the Dabrowa Jews were also the landlords and some professional people. All of them spoke Polish well, using the dialect of the region. In some villages in the District of Dabrowa lived the Jewish farmers.

I was working in a lawyer's office before my bar exam and one event remains engraved in my memory.

In the first days of my professional work an older woman came to me. She had a legal problem and needed advice. The problem was quite complicated and after a long meeting, I explained that, on the whole, her problem could be solved to her advantage if she went to court. The client paid for the advice and said: "Everything is fine, but because my adversary is a Jew, I will first call him to the rabbi." It was the first time that I was in this sort of situation because my client was Catholic. The client recognized my surprise and said:

"We have here a custom that if we, the non-Jews, have a disagreement with a Jew, first we call the Jew to the rabbi. And it is very rarely that we go to court; usually, we reach an agreement through the rabbi."

## II

Later on my client informed me that she had reached an agreement with the Jew through the rabbi.

I found out that many, many times the conflicts between the non-Jews and the Jews in Dabrowa were solved by the rabbi.

I lived in Dabrowa for six months. Later, during the First World War, I visited Dabrowa several times, and after the war when I had occasion to go there, I realized that the conditions of life had not changed.

## III

The year 1942.

The world was in flames.

The Nazis had started the bloody horrors of the war. There was a lot of blood all around, an ocean of blood, and a lot of it Jewish blood.

The Jews were confined to ghettos and they were taken from them to be killed by different methods. This was called the liquidation.

The majority of the Jews from Dabrowa, Zabno, Szczucin, Wojnicz, Debica, Mielec and Tuchow were killed in their own hometowns; however, the remainder were sent to Tarnow. There was a report made by the authorities of the vicinity of Tarnow that all the small towns were *judenfrei* (without Jews).

In the autumn of 1942 there was even the report that Tarnow was *judenfrei* because thousands of Jews were murdered, and only a handful of them were sent to the concentration camps.

## IV

The autumn of 1942 was already advanced. The days were short, but lovely, gay, sunny.

In the market of Dabrowa a few people were walking slowly. In the few stores which had previously belonged to Jews, the new owners did not have much to do. Two vendors stood near their booths and talked loudly.

Suddenly the tranquility of the afternoon was interrupted by the sound of a car. The car stopped in the middle of the marketplace and a few Gestapo men stepped out. Like hunting dogs they looked around and then entered a small restaurant, eager to get some information. A few minutes later they left the restaurant. They looked like hunters ready for hunting. With them was an informer, a *Volksdeutsch* (a Pole who considered himself to be of German origin). At this moment a young man of sixteen approached the car. He winked his little green eyes at the *Volksdeutch* and told him: "I have very interesting news for these gentlemen."

One of the Gestapo men was from Silesia. He spoke Polish, and he went over to the boy and said:

"Talk, but say the truth."

The boy turned around. He pointed with his fingers to the outskirts of town and said:

"There, away from the houses, is an abandoned cave and a few Jews are hiding there."

"What are you saying?" said the Gestapo man. He immediately translated the information to his colleagues.

The other Gestapo men suddenly became animated. They asked the boy "Do you know exactly where it is?"

The boy nodded and added:

"Of course. My mother saw them, and I can show you exactly the place where they hide."

When the Gestapo man from Silesia had explained everything to his colleagues, one of them (apparently their leader), a man around twenty-five whose eyes were angry and wild, exclaimed:

"Again, again. How is it possible? If this is true, I will teach the mayor of this town a lesson. Let's go there immediately."

The boy entered the car with the expression of a hero on his face. He smiled stupidly and showed the directions.

The car moved on.

From the little shops people observed the scene, and one vendor said to another,

"This little hooligan in the Gestapo car will bring a tragedy. How miserable are people in the world today!"

V

After a few minutes, the Gestapo men drove along the limits of the town. There were only a few houses on the road. A little stream ran beside it. The trees were caressed by a gentle breeze which was carrying the last leaves into the air before they fell to the ground. Here and there, the little sparrows fluttered free and gay.

The youngster, the expedition guide, drew the attention of the Gestapo men to a small mound of earth covered with grass, and whispered:

"Here is the old cave, and the Jews hide there."

The Gestapo men quickly jumped out of the car, approached the mound, and looked around carefully. Suddenly they saw a small, wooden door. They drew nearer and one of the Gestapo men kicked the door with his boot and started to scream: "*Aufmachen*" (Open).

Although this order was repeated many times, no sound came from inside. Then another Gestapo man kicked the door very hard and broke it into splinters. Through the light of the penetrating rays of sun, the Gestapo men saw a few silhouettes pressed closely together, bent and trembling with fear. The order was given: "Judenraus," but nobody in the cave moved. Two Gestapo men went inside and blindly beat people with their whips. They dragged the Rabbi Izaak from Dabrowa and a few other Dabrowa Jews from the shelter. Their faces were pale, yellow, anemic—their beards were long and wild.

All the people who were in the cave came out. Each of them, while leaving the cave, tried to straighten his back and then stopped, one near the other, completely motionless. They looked like statues. Every one of them wore his *capota* (a long Hasidic black robe) and a snow-white mortal shirt (when a Jew dies, he is buried wearing only a white robe and a prayer shawl).

The cynical, brutal, savage group of Gestapo men sensed something morbid. The sight of these Jews, tracked down from their hidden place, made a strong impression on them. But this kept them still only a short while. They became acquainted with the vision very fast. One of the Gestapo men placed himself in front of the Jews and, flicking his whip, gave an order to them to form a column, four by four, and to march forward. They were hustled to the cemetery.

There, the last group of the Jews from Dabrowa were asked to dig their own graves. The Jews refused to obey. One of the men condemned to death took a bottle of vodka from the pocket of his long caftan. He took a small sip and offered it to the others to drink. They drank *le' chaim*—to life—to the future life—and then, without paying attention to the screaming of the Gestapo men surrounding them, Rabbi Izaak gave an order, "*Juden tanzt*" (Dance Jews) and started to sing an old Hasidic melody. Among graves and the solemn tranquility of the cemetery an old Hasidic melody with the words "Oy, Oy, Oy, Oy" resounded loudly. It echoed amid the stones of the cemetery, and the Jews joined hands. They danced, they straightened their backs and with their heads high, they danced, they danced an old Hasidic wedding dance.

The Gestapo men were furious. Their threats, shouts, and orders did not awaken any response from the dancing group.

On the one side there was the abominable cowardice of the representatives of the *Herrenvolk*, and on the other side there was the courage, the almost celestial dignity, and the disdain for death of these human beings who were physically weak but morally strong, as is proper for the sons of the old and steadfast nation.

The Gestapo men were astonished. They kept repeating their orders to the Jews to stop dancing. Nobody listened to them.

There was only one leader, one inspiration for the people who danced—the rabbi, Rabbi Izaak. It was Rabbi Izaak who kept repeating, amid the singing, "*Juden tanzt!*" And the Jews, as if in ecstasy, looking heavenward, sang "Oy,Yoy, Oy, Yoy." They sang and danced.

Then one of the Gestapo men took his gun from its case and killed the nearest dancing Jew. The Jew fell, but the others just moved one step back. They again joined their hands; they came closer one to another, and again the voice was heard:

"*Juden tanzt*" and the melody "Oy, Yoy, Oy" continued to ascend into the heavens.

The Jews danced as if a new, supernatural might had come into their weak bodies.

Other Gestapo men followed the example of the first one who had killed the dancing man. They shot left and right. Each time one of the Jews was killed, the others continued to dance.

The revered rabbi was killed, and only two Jews were alive. One shouted to the other, "Tanz Jidel" and this Hasidic dance stopped only when the last Jew was shot.

Rabbi Izaak and his disciples, who danced and sang with their eyes watching the sky, went to the other world. I am sure that when their chanting souls arrived in paradise, they finished their singing with joy in the choir of angels.

The hangmen and killers without scruples had been surprised at this action of the Jews, but not one human sentiment penetrated their hearts. It only enraged them. They felt that they had been humiliated; they felt that the *Herrenvolk* was offended; as well as Hitler, whom they represented.

The Gestapo men decided to avenge themselves devilishly. They kicked and tried to break the bodies of their victims with their boots. And this took place in Europe, in the 20th century, just forty miles from Krakow.

## VI

I dedicate this reminiscence of the Hasidic dance to the future historian as a contribution to the history of so-called humanity.

The above described story is, alas, true, it is not a product or a fantasy of the writer.

Paris, April 1949

# Unsane Tokef

## I

*U*nsane Tokef. The sound of these two words had a very special meaning for, and provoked fear within, every Jew. And the kind of deep piety with which the old *chazzan* (cantor) Josef Majer was singing this prayer was unforgettable.

When somebody watched the chazzan during the prayer, it was impossible to see that the chazzan's spirit was absent from the synagogue—it was as if the chazzan heard the sound of the *shofar hagadol* (great trumpet) played in heaven, and that he was a part of the crowd of celestial angels, proclaiming with him *Hiney Yom Hadin*—The Day of Judgement is here.

When the chazzan reached the second part of the prayer, enumerating the verdicts of heaven for the next year, his voice seemed to be an echo of the celestial proclamation of these verdicts.

For thirty years Josef Majer had been a chazzan, and for thirty years had said the same prayer on Rosh Hashanah and Yom Kippur. Even when he served in the Austrian army during the First World War, from 1914 to 1918, he always assisted the rabbi in this prayer. He would put a long frock and tallis over his uniform and sing for his coreligionists *Unsane Tokef*.

This prayer remained new for him every year, and he prepared himself each time as if it was the first time. Chazzan Majer would think, over and over, of how to make a certain movement or gesture during the singing of the prayer. He studied every nuance of modulation of the voice which would fit the different parts and sentences. At this time the chazzan would forget his everyday problems and worries, and on the Day of Judgement he was singing and saying the prayer in ecstasy as if he were in the ethereal, celestial world.

The choir had many problems with the chazzan during the time of preparation. The members of the choir, adults and youngsters, were not able to appreciate the greatness of every word of the prayer, and did not understand the meaning of assisting the chazzan in its rendering. It required a lot of effort on the part of the chazzan to prepare and to allow the choir to enter the appropriate mood.

The Holy Days, however, were the days of Josef Majer's triumph. He was able to bring all the worshippers to a very special concentration as they prayed together, and later he was highly praised by them.

## II

Chazzan Josef Majer had a very special feeling before the Holy Days of the year 1938 (5699). First of all, the chazzan could not find in this pre-holiday time, any peace of mind. Although he was quite happy that he had discovered and engaged a few new members of the choir, very young boys whose voices were particularly beautiful and seemed to belong to heavenly cherubs; and although he was pleased that his former singer, who for many years had lived in Germany, came back and reported immediately to him upon his arrival; deep in his heart the chazzan worried a lot. He heard about the growing anti-Semitism in the world and the news about ill-treatment of Jews was shocking to the dreaming soul of this artist.

Never before had the *Unsane Tokef* of Josef Majer and his choir made such an impression on the worshippers as in 1938. Nobody ever reacted similarly before.

When Chana Rachel, an old woman, widow of a butcher, found out that the beginning of a prayer in which people should cry took place, she started to lament loudly. With her, all the women sitting in the women's section cried; and afterwards, almost all the men were weeping so loud that at certain moments the chazzan and the choir were not heard.

This was on the first day of Rosh Hashanah of 1938, and it was so on the second day of Rosh Hashanah. On the day of Yom Kippur, people wept even more.

The poor Jews had a reason to weep because on this day of Rosh Hashanah the verdict was written and on the day of Yom Kippur the verdict was sealed— the brown shirted Nazi beasts had started their march across Europe and their extermination of the Jews.

## III

On the first day of Tishri 5700 (September 14, 1939) the Germans were already the masters of the city were Josef Majer lived. The synagogue was razed to the ground because, at the beginning of the Nazi rule, the burning of the synagogues was ordered. The Jews did not have any place to worship, and collective prayer was forbidden. In spite of this a few Jews got together and they prayed in hiding.

The time passed by. More than six million Jews perished, and among them were young and old, men and women, adults and children—they all died different kinds of death. The authors of the *Unsane Tokef* had not foreseen the forms of death which became a part of the Jewish destiny. Oh, irony—at the time when the prayer *Unsane Tokef* was composed, the culture was not as high as in the twentieth century.

IV

After 1939, the chazzan Josef Majer never sang the *Unsane Tokef* again. During Rosh Hashanah and Yom Kippur in 1940 he worked very hard for the Germans, and in August, 1941, he was shot together with many thousands of Jews.

Today, during the Holy Days when I, the survivor of the terrible war, one of so very few, hear the *Unsane Tokef*, I remember Josef Majer of blessed memory.

When the words "*Umalachin yechufezun*" are uttered, when "*Hiney Yom Hadin*" is proclaimed, I believe, as I listen to the words of the prayer, that somewhere far away, among the angels dwells Josef Majer, the chazzan, the artist, the singer, and the dreamer.

# Kol Nidrei

He is forty-two years old.

During the First World War, being only seventeen, he was drafted by the Austrian army. When in service, he fought at the side of the German ally for the victory of Germany and for the growth of the power. He was not able to contribute to this victory, because the Germans lost the war, but he kept two mementos of it: a small war-time gold medal and the scars of a serious injury.

Today he is forty-two, but hollow-cheeked, bald with just remnants of grey hair, his three front teeth knocked out by the Nazis, and grey stubble on his face—he looks sixty-five.

He has been in Auschwitz for fifteen months. He was granted a special favor on the day when the Jews were killed in the ghetto where he used to live (so that it could be reported to be *Judenfrei*): he was selected with several dozen other men for labor.

Before he was taken to Auschwitz, he was in several other places of torture, the so-called labor camps. There is not one spot on his whole body where he has not been beaten and bruised.

Today is the 9th day of October, 1943. To him it is the 9th day of Tishrei in the year 5704.

He has felt uneasy all day today. He worked poorly and was badly beaten by the Gestapo man who was watching the prisoners.

Today is Erev Yom Kippur.

All day his thoughts have been in the past. With his mind's eyes he can see the whole family seated at the afternoon meal in his parents' house. This meal is served earlier than usual on the day before Yom Kippur to have plenty of room and appetite for the dinner which immediately precedes the fasting. The dinner has to take one through about twenty-six hours. Then he went to the synagogue for the *minhah* with his father, and the rest of the family went with them.

He remembers his mother, his three brothers, and two sisters. None of them, nor any of their relatives, is alive today. His father died shortly before the war, and as for the rest of the family—his mother, brothers, and sisters and their families were murdered by the Nazi bandits.

His further recollections are stopped by four lashes of the Gestapo man's whip.

He continues to work.

What was it like a few years ago? He carries on the interrupted thoughts. He was married. Oh, what a good woman, an ideal Jewish wife and mother was his beloved one! And how nice and beautiful were his children! Two boys and two little girls.

The Nazis killed them during an operation as they called those organized mass murders.

His head has been full of these ponderings and recollections all day long as he worked and on his way from work to camp.

It is five o'clock in the afternoon, the time of the last daily suffering.

Sunset is near, the end of the day; it is getting dark.

The thoughtful Jew is standing in the right wing of the second row. The stubborn thoughts that have been coming upon him all day are not leaving. His recollections again take him to the fairyland of his quiet past.

At that time he would have been in the synagogue with his family and the cantor would have just been finishing singing "*Kol Nidrei*" for the third time.

He can hear the old, melancholic, deep melody that always seems to fascinate every Jew, and he seems to hear the final words: *Ushvuatanah lah shvuot!*

Now, staring away, that miserable shadow of man silently repeats to himself the words of another fervent prayer to the Creator: "*Vnislach lechol adas benei Israel.*"

At this moment the Gestapo man standing in front of the prisoners notices that the convict is not looking straight ahead as the regulations demand, but that he is looking upwards with a strange expression on his face. What disrespect!

He runs up to him and yells: *Du verfluchter Saujude, wohin schaust Du? Weisst Du nicht, wo Du bist?!*'' (You damn Jew, where are you looking? Don't you know where you are?!)—but there is no reaction, the prisoner is not paying any attention to the screams; he cannot feel the man's nearness. His soul is somewhere else because at this moment he is saying the prayer with the cantor, asking the Lord for the remission of sins, for forgiveness: "*V'hager hagar btocham.*"

The infuriated Gestapo man hits the prisoner hard on the head, with a thick baton. The skull breaks and the falling man's brain pours out—the brain whose last notion was a prayer for forgiveness: "*V'hager hagar btocham*". And it is with that prayer, for the Nazi torturer's sins to be forgiven, that his pure soul stands before the throne of the Eternal.

Paris, June 22. 1949

# Die Jidishe Mame (The Jewish Mother)

Mama. This is the most beautiful expression in the vocabulary of all languages of the world. Mama gives life to a human being and lives with her child even before she gives birth. Later she gives her breast to the child, at the moment that this child comes into the world. The word "mama" comes from the Latin "mamma" which means the breast.

From the moment a child is born, the eye of a mother (mother—the nurse, the caretaker, the guardian angel) watches the child all his life. The first word usually babbled or wailed is "mama," and later, in adult life, often in tears or suffering or sorrow, the word "mama" is heard, and the sentence, "Oh—mama, if you were with me."

When a woman is giving birth, in the most difficult moment, often from her lips comes the word "Mama." She would ask her mother to help her because a mother never deceives her child and you can trust her blindly. You can always find a refuge, a defense and safe harbor in your mother. Sometimes when people die, their last thoughts go back to mother, to this one who gave birth, and often people call, "Mother," in the last moments of their lives.

With rare exceptions, all mothers are symbols of goodness and heart, disinterested love and warmth, nobility, and the capacity for limitless sacrifices.

Among the mothers of the world, the Jewish mothers played a very important role as those who were able to sacrifice a lot for their people—people persecuted throughout the ages, tortured in different places of the world. *Die Jidische Mame* became an ideal of a very special mother.

During the tragic storm, the Second World War, the hundreds of thousands of Jewish mothers gave examples of limitless love. They were often sacrificing their lives trying to save their children from extermination.

This is the story of one mother.

This story was told to me by a son—Jozef Rebhun from Przemysl.

The tracks on the rail line of Jaroslaw-Belz were overloaded. During the days and nights the brown Nazi beasts were transporting in tightly closed cattle cars hundreds of thousands of Jews. They were directed to the extermination camp in Belz. Who were these people in the transports? They were old and young, men and women, without any distinction of sex or age. This was their last journey, similar to the horrible entrance to hell.

In one of these transports were young Jozef and his mother.

After they passed Jaroslaw, the mother started to talk to her son.

"You, my child, you have to try to save your life—you are young—you have to live."

Afterwards, she revealed to him her plan in the vicinity of the forest which they were supposed to pass.

"You have to open the door very quietly—you will jump, and run to the forest—I will jump after you. I will be nearer to the train and easier for the guards to reach, which will direct all their attention to me. In the meantime you will reach the forest, and with God's help, you will be safe."

The mother didn't give any time for her son to think. After a while, she very discreetly opened the door, she pushed her son to the door, and asked him to jump. The son jumped from the train, and immediately after him jumped his mother. Jozef found himself in the forest. The bullets of the Nazis killed his mother. She died heroically on the battlefield, but she saved her son who hid in the thicket of the forest and who afterwards, struggling every day, survived the war.

*Die Jidische Mame*—the Jewish mother. To you and those similar to you, for the mothers who sacrificed their lives to save the lives of their children, we owe respect and glory. We bow to you and to the blessed memory of the true Jewish mothers.

Paris, February 2. 1951

# Biographical Notes

Emil Goldman, his wife, Mila, and Mila's mother perished in the vicinity of Brzezany.

Leon Goldman died on a cart during the deportation from Kalne to Kozowa in 1943. His wife, Pepcia, his sons, Salo and Bunio and his daughter, Hanusia were killed by Nazis. Adela-Ada survived. She lives in Israel. She is married to Shimon Mayer. They have two daughters, Pnina and Ariela.

Rozia-Ziuta Goldman-Weber was arrested in front of the store where she waited for her ration of potatoes. She was denounced by her former colleague, a Polish nurse. Rozia was kept in Brigitki prison in Lwow for a short time and later was killed by the Nazis. Her husband, Bertek-Bronislaw Weber, survived.

Benio Goldman and Gusta Szwadron were first helped by Ukrainian peasants, who promised to save them. However, later on the Ukrainians changed their mind and killed Benio and Gusta in the vicinity of Kalne.

Ginia Goldman was killed in Brzezany in 1942 or 1943.

Lunia Birman-Goldman and Gizela-Dzidzia Goldman, the daughter of Lunia and Dr. Samuel Goldman, lost their lives in Auschwitz in 1942 or 1943. Dr. Samuel Goldman survived. He remarried and emigrated to Israel in 1948. Dr. Goldman worked as a physician to the end of his life. He died in 1977.

Regina Herzig was killed by Nazis in Debica in 1941 or 1943.

Lonus Herzig was killed in the English prisoners camp during a raid in Germany in 1944.

Hela Zarski-Schorr and Wlodek (Zev) Schorr, the son of Hela and Zygmunt Schorr, were denounced by a Pole. They were taken to prison and were later killed in Lwow in 1943.

Zygmunt Schorr (Sigmond Shore) survived the war. He remarried. With his second wife, Rena-Lena Herzig (Lena Allen-Shore), he had two sons, Michel Maria Joseph and Jacques Jean Meor. He died in 1967 in Montreal, Canada. Lena Allen-Shore lives in Philadelphia; Michel M. J. Shore and Jacques J. M. Shore live in Ottawa, Canada.

Michal Schorr and his wife, Rela, were killed in the vicinity of Kolomyja. They died in an old barn, apparently during a fire set by Nazis.

Klara Schorr-Kanfer and Ritka Kanfer, the daughter of Klara and Dr. Leon Kanfer, were shot and killed before the eyes of Dr. Kanfer. Dr. Kanfer attacked the Nazis who came to take his wife and his child away. This happened in Kolomyja in 1943.

Dr. Leon (Lonek) Kanfer lost his life after fighting with two Gestapo men who came to take away his wife, Klara, and his daughter, Ritka. He was bitten to death by Gestapo dogs.

Maria (Marysia) Schorr-Procek was taken away from the railway station in Stanislawow or Kolomyja in 1943. She never came back. Her husband searched for her a long time. Nobody knows how she was killed or where.

Hermann (Hesio) Neuschuller, his mother and two sisters, Pola and Frydzia, were killed on June 10 or 12, 1943, in Brzezany. Hesio was offered life but he didn't want to see his mother and sisters die and he decided to share their fate.

Runia Herzig-Bross and her husband, Maurycy (Morek) Bross, were killed by Nazis in Krzemieniec in 1943.

Thea (Tusia) Bross and her brother, Jozef Bross, the children of Runia and Maurycy Bross, were killed in Krzemieniec in 1943.

Igo Schoenfeld disappeared in 1943 or 1944.

Karolina Rubel and her husband, Robert Rubel, were killed by Nazis in Kolomyja in 1942 or 1943.

Lonek Rubel was killed by Nazis in Lwow in 1944.

Frydek Rubel survived the war. He died in Australia in 1974.

Mundek Rubel survived the war. He died in Israel in 1976.

Izek (Teddy) Rubel survived the war. He is a physician and lives with his wife, Dr. Terry Rubel, in Fort Salonga, L.I., N.Y. They have one son, Ray.

Jadwiga (Jadzia) Rosenfeld was killed by Nazis in Jaslo in 1942 or 1943.

Stefan (Stefus) Eibschutz was killed by Nazis in Lwow in 1942 or 1943.

Dr. Jakub Herzig, his wife, Lusia Goldman-Herzig, their daughter, Rena-Lena, and their son, Adam, survived the war. Dr. J. Herzig died in 1956 in Montreal, Canada. Lusia Goldman-Herzig died in 1967 in Montreal, Canada. Their daughter, Rena-Lena, lives in Philadelphia. Their son, Adam, lives in Philadelphia.

# A Note About the Authors

DR. JAKUB O. HERZIG was born in Stryj, Poland. He received his degree of Doctor of Law from the University of Lwow. From 1919 to 1939 he practiced law and was a well-known criminal lawyer and dedicated community leader, active in humanitarian and charitable organizations.

Profoundly concerned with human rights, he was appalled at the apparently unchallenged rise of Hitler and the methods he used to attain power. Early in 1939 he wrote a motion picture script against Hitler which was scheduled to begin production in the fall. The events of September of that year made it impossible.

Jakub Herzig survived the horrors of World War II in Poland with his wife and two children. He had been active in the underground resistance.

In 1946 he emigrated to Paris, France, and from there in 1952 to Montreal, Canada. In Paris and Montreal he devoted his time entirely to writing. He wrote novels, dramas, short stories and articles which appeared in French and Canadian newspapers and periodicals. In Paris in 1947 he was editor of the *Bulletin*.

Among his works were the following:

*Nous ne sommes pas des heros* (We are not heroes), Paris, 1947

*With Honor*, Paris, 1950

*Macevot*, short stories, Paris, 1949, 1950

*Black Devil*, Montreal, 1955

*Steps in the Journey of the War* (Memoirs), Montreal, 1955

*Jaslo*, Montreal, 1955

*The Wrecked Life*, Montreal, 1955

*Steps in the Journey of the War* and *Jaslo* received the award for "Special Distinction" from Yad Vashem and were published in Israel.

Jakub O. Herzig died in 1956 in Montreal. A prominent defender of justice, he devoted his time, mind and heart to this end. He wrote about those who had suffered and died unnecessarily because of injustice, in the hope that by commemorating their lives, he might help to prevent future wrongs.

DR. LENA ALLEN-SHORE was born in Poland. She was active in the underground movement during World War II. After the war she studied economics, law, political science and music in Poland and France and sociology, education and philosophy in Canada and the United States. She received her M.A. degree in education from McGill University in Montreal in 1972 and her Ph.D. degree in philosophy from Dropsie University in Philadelphia in 1980.

Lena Allen-Shore is the author of poems, songs, essays, and a novel that has been published in Europe, Canada and the United States.

Among her works are the following:

*L'Orage dans mon coeur* (poems), Editions du Lys, Montreal, 1963

*Le Pain de la Paix* (poems), Editions du Lys, Montreal, 1964

*Ne me demandez pas qui je suis* (novel), La Quebecoise, Montreal, 1965

*May the Flowers Grow* (poems), Shengold Publishers, New York, 1969

*Langue Universelle (Fraternite et culture)* (essay on education), Aries, Montreal, 1971

*The Singing God—Le Dieu qui chante* (poems), Aries, Montreal, 1971

*Le Pain de la Paix* brought her the admiration of Dr. Albert Schweitzer, who wrote her what is considered the last letter in his own hand.

Allen-Shore's poems and articles have appeared in various French and English newspapers. She has read her poetry and sung her songs on radio and television.

Her poem, ''Le testament de John F. Kennedy,'' is included in an anthology of French-Canadian writers published in France.

Lena Allen Shore is currently a Senior Research Fellow at the University of Pennsylvania, School of Social Work.